HOMETO...

SHIPMENT 5

His Best Friend's Baby by Molly O'Keefe
Caleb's Bride by Wendy Warren
Her Sister's Secret Life by Pamela Toth
Lori's Little Secret by Christine Rimmer
High-Stakes Bride by Fiona Brand
Hometown Honey by Kara Lennox

SHIPMENT 6

Reining in the Rancher by Karen Templeton
A Man to Rely On by Cindi Myers
Your Ranch or Mine? by Cindy Kirk
Mother in Training by Marie Ferrarella
A Baby for the Bachelor by Victoria Pade
The One She Left Behind by Kristi Gold
Her Son's Hero by Vicki Essex

SHIPMENT 7

Once and Again by Brenda Harlen
Her Sister's Fiancé by Teresa Hill
Family at Stake by Molly O'Keefe
Adding Up to Marriage by Karen Templeton
Bachelor Dad by Roxann Delaney
It's That Time of Year by Christine Wenger

SHIPMENT 8

The Rancher's Christmas Princess by Christine Rimmer
Their Baby Miracle by Lillian Darcy
Mad About Max by Penny McCusker
No Ordinary Joe by Michelle Celmer
The Soldier's Baby Bargain by Beth Kery
A Texan Under the Mistletoe by Leah Vale

HOMETOWN HEARTS

Unexpected Bride

LISA CHILDS

⬡HARLEQUIN® HOMETOWN HEARTS

Recycling programs
for this product may
not exist in your area.

ISBN-13: 978-0-373-21461-7

Unexpected Bride

Copyright © 2008 by Lisa Childs-Theeuwes

Printed in U.S.A.

www.Harlequin.com

Ever since **Lisa Childs** read her first romance novel (a Harlequin story, of course) at age eleven, all she wanted was to be a romance writer. With over forty novels published with Harlequin, Lisa is living her dream. She is an award-winning, bestselling romance author. Lisa loves to hear from readers, who can contact her on Facebook, through her website, lisachilds.com, or her snail-mail address, PO Box 139, Marne, MI 49435.

With great appreciation to Jennifer Green for encouraging me to write a Harlequin American Romance proposal, to Kathleen Scheibling for accepting that proposal for The Wedding Party series and to all the brides who included me in their wedding parties.

Chapter One

Clayton McClintock pressed his cell phone to his ear. "I'm going to be late," he told his date, as he studied the flight schedule posted in the terminal. All the flights were on time but one. *Hers*. It figured. Conversation swirled around him as people rushed through the arrival gates and met those waiting for them in the lounge area.

On his phone there was dead silence. He pulled the cell from his ear to study its small screen, but his call hadn't been lost. "Ellen, are you there?" he asked.

"Yes," was the reply, in a tone of long-suffering patience, followed by a sigh reminiscent of the dramatic ones his sisters had subjected him to in their teens. "This isn't working, Clayton. You stand me up more often than you see me."

He sighed, too—with frustration. "Things have been crazy with my sister's wedding stuff." Writing checks, that had been his primary duty. And then he'd been pressed into playing chauffeur. Everyone else was busy with the rehearsal this afternoon.

He glanced at his watch. If Abby's flight was any later, they'd miss dinner as well as the activities at the church. His plan had been to pick up his date after the rehearsal and bring her with him to the dinner. This wasn't the first time he'd had to set aside his own plans for the sake of his family, though.

"Things *have* been crazy," Ellen agreed. "And your brother…"

Rory, who was in his teens, was going through a difficult time right now, also reminding Clayton of *her*. But she was hardly a teenager anymore. People grew up and matured—probably even Abby Hamilton. Clayton had to believe that Rory would do the same, provided his big brother didn't kill him first.

"It's always something with your family,

Clayton," Ellen said. "You never have time for me."

He couldn't argue with her. He didn't have time for himself, either. Not with his job and his brother and sisters and his mom. How had his dad managed everything? Clayton had taken over family responsibilities eight years ago, and he had yet to figure out how to handle everything his father had managed so effortlessly. He lifted a hand and wiped it over his eyes. He was tired.

"I've known for some time that it wasn't going to work out, Clayton. So don't bother calling me anymore."

"My sister's getting married tomorrow." That would take care of one responsibility. "Things will get better then."

"How? Is she taking your mom and sister and brother with her? You don't have room in your life for me or for any woman, Clayton. I'm sorry."

The phone clicked and the call ended, not because of a faulty connection but because of a lack of a romantic connection. And except for going stag to the rehearsal dinner and the wedding, he wasn't even too upset. Clayton hadn't dated anyone long enough to say that he'd ever had a serious relationship. He blew out a ragged breath of relief. He didn't want a serious relationship because it was just one more responsibility he didn't need.

Waiting in an airport for Abby was bad enough. How like her to fly in at the last moment. Some bridesmaid she'd turned out to be. Fortunately Molly had asked her longtime friend, Brenna Kelly, to be maid of honor. Clayton couldn't imagine Abby handling the responsibilities.

He headed over to the airport coffee shop and filled a disposable cup with strong black brew. When he passed his money to the clerk, he ignored her flirty smile and bright eyes. Maybe he'd stop dating for a while—it wasn't as if he ever intended to get married, anyway. He'd leave that to Molly, Colleen and Rory. Heck, he wouldn't even mind if his mom got married again. It was already eight years since his dad had died.

The same length of time Abby Hamilton had been gone. She'd taken off right after the funeral, even skipping her high school graduation. Not that she'd have been able to graduate with her class, since she'd just been expelled. If Clayton didn't get a handle on Rory soon, the youngest McClintock would probably be heading down that same dead end.

What was she doing now? His sisters and mom kept in touch with her, but they didn't tell him much. They knew how he felt. The last he'd heard, she was moving around, working temp jobs, which didn't surprise him. Nothing had ever seemed to hold her interest for long.

"Flight 3459 is arriving at Gate B4."

The announcement startled him and his hand jerked, spilling coffee over his fingers and burning them. Abby was back. Clayton's stomach lurched, maybe from the bitter liquid, or maybe because he knew that Abby Hamilton had always been nothing but trouble. She might be older now, and maybe even wiser, but he doubted she had changed that much.

He stared over the heads of other people gathered who waited to meet the late arrivals. They greeted each other with exuberant hugs and voices full of excitement. Somehow he doubted Abby would be that happy to see him—she had no idea he'd been called into service as her chauffeur.

He glanced in the direction of the approaching passengers. Where was she? Everyone moved toward the luggage carousel, its gears grinding as it began a slow rotation. Then metal clunked and the bags began to drop onto the carousel. Clayton ran his hand, which still stung from the coffee burn, across his face. Somehow the ground crew had gotten the luggage off the plane before she'd disembarked. Now, there was no hope of their making the rehearsal. He'd have to push her, in order to make the dinner.

So she hadn't changed. He caught sight of her, finally, first spotting her fair hair as she strolled into view behind a group of stragglers pushing strollers. Until the others moved toward their luggage, he could barely see her. She probably wasn't much over five feet tall. As she got closer, he studied her face, which was framed by a wild mass of curls. Her eyes shone a bright, clear blue between thick fringes of black lashes.

Clayton's gaze traveled down her body, clad in a ribbed white tank top and tight faded jeans. His stomach lurched again. Abby was still going to be trouble; probably much more trouble as a woman than she'd been as a kid.

Then he noticed that her right hand was wrapped around another smaller hand. At her side walked a little girl of about four or five. With her own blond curls and those same bright eyes, she was the spitting image of her mother. His breath left his lungs as the shock slammed through him.

No one had told him that Abby Hamilton had a child.

Abby glanced around the airport, looking for Molly or Colleen or Brenna, and then her gaze collided with Clayton McClintock's. His chocolate-brown eyes were wide with surprise. He rubbed a hand over his eyes as if he didn't believe what he was seeing. Then the hand skimmed down his face, over sharp cheekbones and a square jaw. He didn't look much different at thirty than he had at twenty-two, except that he wasn't boyishly thin anymore. His black knit polo shirt strained across his chest and upper arms, and stone-colored khakis encased his long legs. Clayton McClintock was all man now.

Abby exhaled deeply, stirring her bangs so that strands of hair tangled in her lashes. "Oh, no…"

"What's wrong, Mommy?" her daughter asked as she gave her mother a tug.

Abby's feet stopped moving—she didn't want to get any closer to Clayton. No one had told him about Lara. While Abby appreciated her friends' loyalty, she wouldn't have minded if they'd broken their promise not to tell anyone in Cloverville about her daughter. Why had she made them pledge their silence in the first place? She wasn't ashamed of being a single mom. But a part of her was still eighteen, hurting from the disapproval of the townspeople. And no one in Cloverville had disapproved of her more than Clayton.

If only she'd worn one of her tailored business suits instead of her most casual outfit, but now it was too late to change either her clothes or Clayton's opinion of her.

He walked toward them, eating up the short distance with just a couple of strides. "Abby."

She drew in a breath and then pasted on a smile. "Clayton."

"It's been a long time," he said, his gaze hard as he stared at her.

Not long enough. He obviously didn't want her back in Cloverville any more than she wanted to be back.

Then his head dipped, and his gaze softened on her little girl. His throat moved as he swallowed, and then he asked, "So who's this pretty young lady?"

"My daughter."

"I can tell," he said, his lips curving into a warm smile that etched creases into his cheeks.

Abby's pulse quickened. She couldn't remember if she'd ever seen him smile before. Lara, however, was more frightened than charmed and ducked behind her mother's legs, grasping Abby's hand tightly with one hand as she clutched a well-loved teddy bear with the other.

"You don't have to be scared," she assured her daughter, even though she'd spent much of her childhood fearing her friends' older brother. But she'd grown up many, many years ago—she'd had no choice. "Clayton isn't a stranger. I've known him a long time. Well, I knew him a long time ago."

"I knew your mother when she was your age," Clayton said as he dropped to his haunches, his slacks pulled taut across muscular thighs. "You look exactly like she did the first time she followed my sister Molly home."

Like a stray dog. That was how he'd always seen her. But then he hadn't been all that wrong. She used to come to the McClintock house with her clothes dirty, her knees scraped and her stomach growling with hunger. And his mom had always cleaned her up and fed her. Mrs. Mick, as Abby had always called her, had been more of a mother to Abby than her own sad excuse for a mother had been. *Mom* had spent more time in the bar than at home, and Abby's dad had always been gone because he drove a semitruck for a living.

"What's your name?" he asked the child.

The small girl whispered her response. "Lara."

"Lara?" Clayton glanced up at Abby.

She nodded, then confirmed what he had to be thinking. "Lara *Hamilton*."

He straightened up. "So you're not married."

"Nope. The closest I'm getting to an altar is Molly's wedding tomorrow." The one reason she had come back to Cloverville: she was going to watch her friend make the biggest mistake of her life, unless somehow she could manage to talk Molly out of it. If not for all the projects Abby had had going on in the past couple of months, she would have come back to Cloverville much sooner. She hoped she had enough time to talk Molly out of the wedding. "I'm sorry you were sent to get me, Clayton. I thought one of the others…"

"They're already at the rehearsal."

She glanced at her watch, then closed her eyes. "We're late."

He probably held her responsible for the computer problems at O'Hare that had delayed their flight. She blamed herself, too, for not coming in earlier. But Clayton was one of the reasons she hadn't wanted to come back to Cloverville at all. No matter what she'd accomplished since she'd left, everyone here—and especially Clayton—would always see her as the poor, screwed-up Hamilton kid who'd been failing high school even before she'd been expelled for malicious mischief and vandalism.

"Is it too late for me to be the flower girl, Mommy?" Lara asked.

Abby's lids lifted, her gaze on her daughter's concerned expression. Lara had been looking forward to her "job" in Molly's wedding, and she'd be disappointed if Abby convinced her friend to cancel.

Clayton turned back to Lara, too, offering reassurance before her mother had a chance to speak. "No, honey, the wedding is tomorrow, and you're going to be the most beautiful flower girl Cloverville has ever seen." He closed one dark eye in a wink, his lashes brushing his cheek.

Abby's heart fluttered. It had to be an aftereffect of flying. Not that she was an anxious flyer. Nope, the nerves were because she was here, less than an hour away from the Cloverville city limits.

"But we do need to get to the rehearsal," Clayton continued. "So we know what to do tomorrow. And after the rehearsal, we're having dinner at Mr. and Mrs. Kelly's. They own the bakery and they always have lots of goodies around, including the best cookies in the world."

Lara tugged on Abby's hand. "Can I have a cookie, Mommy?"

Abby nodded. Even though it would be awfully close to Lara's bedtime when the rehearsal concluded, if it wasn't finished already, sugar didn't affect Lara as it did her mother.

"I'll get your bags and we'll be on our way," Clayton said as he headed toward the carousel.

Abby rushed after him, pulling Lara along with her. She didn't want to accept his help. She really should have rented a car, but Brenna Kelly, the maid of honor and one of Abby's oldest and closest friends, had insisted that it would be easier and faster for someone to pick her up from the airport. "I'll get my own bags, Clayton. You don't know what my suitcases look like."

"I imagine they're the only ones that are left," he said with a smug smile, turning toward the conveyor.

Abby clenched her free hand into a fist and wished she had something to whip at the back of his head. Clayton McClintock had always irritated the heck out of her, with his smug I-have-everything-under-control personality. Why had her friends sent *him* to get the two of them? Just how crazy had this wedding made everyone?

"He's nice, Mommy."

Clayton McClintock was a lot of things. Judgmental, humorless and uptight. But he was *not* nice. While all the other McClintocks had always accepted her as one of the family, Clayton made her feel as if she didn't belong.

Then again, she really hadn't. But most of the time when she was growing up, she'd had no place else to go.

"Mommy?"

She blinked, then gazed down at Lara. "What, honey?"

"Don't you like Clayton?"

She turned to watch him lift their suitcases from the carousel, his impressive biceps straining his shirtsleeves. Then she lied to her daughter for the first time in her life. "Sure I do."

Clayton stood only a few feet away. Despite the grinding of the conveyor belt, he heard her and smothered a laugh. Abby had *never* liked him, which was fine with him. She'd been such a brat in her day. Her daughter might look exactly like her, but apparently she acted nothing like the wild child her mother had been.

"I wouldn't let them leave again," a male voice commented near Clayton's shoulder.

He glanced over at a gray-haired man who was standing beside him. "Excuse me?"

"Your wife and daughter," the older man said, gesturing toward Abby and Lara. "I flew in from Chicago with them."

Clayton's mouth went dry, too dry for him to respond and correct the misconception. His wife and daughter? He'd never take a wife, never have children of his own. That was one plan he didn't intend to let his family change.

"Despite the computer problems at the airport, they stayed so sweet and patient. They're beautiful," the stranger continued. "You're a lucky man."

Clayton simply nodded, not wasting any time with explanations. They were already late. After the rehearsal dinner he would dump Abby, her daughter and suitcases at his mother's house, and his responsibilities to her would be over.

"Slow down, Clayton," Abby said. Sun-streaked fields and dappled woods whipped past the windows of the hybrid SUV. She turned toward the backseat, where Lara's head bobbed in her sleep with each bump in the road. Less than a foot of console separated Abby from Clayton's broad shoulder. His jaw was rigidly set as he stared straight ahead at the road leading into Cloverville.

He hadn't even heard her request. She reached over and touched his thigh. Muscles flexed beneath her fingers and the SUV surged forward as his foot pressed harder on the accelerator.

"Clayton, slow down!" she whispered, not wanting to wake her daughter, even though Lara could sleep anywhere and through anything.

"Grabbing my leg isn't going to slow me down," he said tersely, as he eased off the gas. "It's actually a good way to wind up in the ditch."

Fingers tingling, Abby snatched back her hand and knotted her fingers in her lap.

"Sorry. I didn't mean to startle you, but you didn't hear me."

"Telling me to slow down?" he said. "I thought you were kidding, considering the way you drive. You thrive on speed."

"I used to," she admitted. Although speed had had little to do with her poor driving. Undiagnosed attention deficit disorder had been the real reason for her erratic youthful driving—that and bad brakes.

"Did having a kid finally settle you down?"

Diet and exercise had gotten the ADD under control, but nothing had affected her as much as becoming a mother. "Yes," she agreed.

"Responsibility will do that to you," he said, his voice thick with bitterness.

She'd always figured that after he'd mourned the loss of his father, he'd enjoyed stepping into the patriarch's shoes and taking control of his family. Even before his dad had gotten sick, Clayton had bossed his younger siblings and Abby around so much that they'd all looked forward to his leaving for college.

Maybe his bitterness was because he'd never gotten over his father's death. It had affected all their lives so much. "Clayton…"

He turned his head slightly, his gaze skimming over her. The tingling spread from her fingertips throughout her body in reaction to that look. *What the heck was that about?* He'd never looked at her like that when they were younger, when she'd secretly wished he would; wished that he'd return from college and notice that she was all grown up.

"What?" he asked when she remained silent with remembered self-disgust. In the end, she'd actually missed him when he'd gone away to college. She doubted he'd missed her at all these past eight years.

She expelled a soft, shaky sigh. "So are you speeding to the church?"

He shook his head. "When I went to get the car, I called Brenna's cell. Reverend Howland had another commitment and couldn't wait any longer, so they had to rehearse without the missing members of the party."

"Us," she acknowledged, bracing herself for his accusatory stare. He'd always blamed her for any trouble his sisters had gotten into. Like the tattoos, for instance. But in Abby's opinion, this wedding was the most trouble Molly had ever gotten into, and she wanted to get her out.

"We weren't the only ones who missed the

rehearsal," Clayton admitted. "Neither the best man nor Eric was there."

"Eric." Eric South been the lone male member of a group of friends that included Abby, Brenna Kelly, Molly and Molly's sister, Colleen, who was a few years younger than the classmates. "I hope he makes it to the dinner." He could help Abby talk Molly out of marrying a stranger.

"I hope *we* do," Clayton muttered as he pressed down on the accelerator.

Abby lifted her hand from her lap but stopped herself from reaching across the console again. "I'm surprised an insurance agent would drive so fast. I remember the lecture about driving responsibly that Mr. Mick gave me when I got my license."

"You listened?" he asked, sounding surprised. Probably remembering his father's patented lecture himself, he slowed down.

"Since you run the agency now, do you give the safe-driving speech, too?" she asked.

He nodded. "At the high school and the office."

Just as his father had done. Had Clayton chosen to be an insurance agent or had he just assumed the job when he'd taken over his father's business after he died? She couldn't ask something so personal. They weren't friends nor were they ever likely to be.

"The Kellys always make plenty of food." She doubted that had changed. "Why are you in such a hurry to get back to Cloverville? Do you have to pick up a date for the dinner?"

Under his breath, he muttered, "Not anymore."

Her lips twitched into a smile. Apparently even the Clayton McClintocks of the world got dumped. "Then you just don't want to be alone with me."

He didn't deny her assumption. "How long are you planning on staying?"

Obviously he didn't want her in Cloverville any more than she wanted to be back. Since he'd slowed down, the scenery enveloped them. Fields and woods, trees thick with green leaves gave way to subdivisions crowded with new houses, streets lined with strip malls, box stores and fast-food restaurants. "This is Cloverville?"

"It's grown since you've been away. Did you think it would stay the same?"

She shook her head. "Nothing stays the same." She'd learned that at a young age. Sadly enough, so had Lara—it was time for Abby to put down roots for the two of them. To give her daughter a home they would live in for more than a year or two. Time to establish permanent headquarters for the temporary employment agency Abby owned. Abby had already given up her apartment in Chicago. She'd been so busy packing that she couldn't fly in sooner. Now she just had to decide on where she and her daughter would settle.

It was only the two of them. The moment Abby had gotten pregnant Lara's father had wanted nothing to do with either of them. Almost five years later, the hurt had faded, but she couldn't fathom how she'd been so wrong about him. She'd thought he'd been such a nice, responsible guy, but maybe it wasn't his fault he couldn't love her. Her own parents hadn't.

Clayton turned the SUV onto Main Street, where nothing had changed. Mrs. Hild's Cape Cod still crowded the corner lot, her prize roses climbing over the carved wooden sign denoting the Cloverville city limits. In the middle of the block was Mr. Carpenter's hardware store, the windows ablaze with the reflection of the setting sun. They also passed the McClintock Insurance Agency, the same gold logo on the front door as the one embroidered on Clayton's shirt. The three-story redbrick building that housed the agency was one of the biggest on the block, taller and wider than the diner and pharmacy flanking it. A For Lease sign had been posted in the window of the first-floor office next to the insurance agency.

"Dr. Strover moved?" she asked.

"He retired," Clayton said. "So I'm looking for a new tenant."

Clayton's dad had owned the building, and now it was Clayton's responsibility—like so many others he'd taken on at twenty-two years of age. The same age Abby had been when she became a mother.

"I was hoping Josh would put his practice there, but his partner thought they needed more space. They're putting up a new building on the west side of Cloverville, closer to Grand Rapids and the hospitals."

"Josh?" she asked, not following his conversation, probably because she was so surprised he was making the effort to talk to her. Eight years ago, except for one night, he'd never bothered to say much of anything to her other than an occasional curt, "Don't you have a home?"

She hadn't then. Or now. She glanced into the backseat where Lara still slept peacefully, her curls tangled around her face. Love filled Abby's heart. Until she'd had her baby, she'd never known how much love one could feel.

"Dr. Josh Towers is the man Molly's marrying tomorrow. I thought you and my sister kept in close contact," he said with a hint of his old disapproval. As if he didn't understand why Molly would want to remain in contact with her. "You don't know the name of her fiancé?"

"Molly and I talk every day either by phone or e-mail." And she'd hardly mentioned her fiancé. Of course, Molly had only just gotten engaged—to a man she obviously didn't love. Not that Abby knew anything about love except what she felt for her daughter. "Don't you think it's too soon?"

"What?"

"The wedding. They hardly know each other."

The muscles in his arm rippled as he gripped the steering wheel. "Since her first year of college, Molly has worked summers at the hospital where he's on staff. She's known him a long time."

"No, she hasn't. They've only just started dating." Frustration churned Abby's stomach. She'd tried to talk to Molly, tried to convince her to wait before she leaped into something as serious as marriage. Molly wasn't the type to act impetuously—she'd always been as responsible as her older brother. "I thought *you,* of all people, would be against this shotgun wedding."

"It's hardly that."

"You've always been so practical, so…"

"Boring?" he finished for her, a muscle jumping in his jaw. He knew how she'd seen him in the past, and he could only imagine what she thought of him now since she'd lived in big cities and he'd stayed here. In Cloverville. Not that he cared what she thought of him. His concern was for Molly. Abby couldn't be right about the wedding. Molly was too smart, too responsible to act as impulsively as Abby always had.

"Judgmental," she answered.

The comment stung, even though it shouldn't have, even though he knew she was only trying to get a rise out of him, just as she always had. No matter how hard he'd tried, she'd made it impossible for him to ignore her.

"I'm judgmental? Really?" he challenged her, then pointed out, "I haven't said anything about…" He lifted his gaze to the rearview mirror, which reflected back the image of her daughter. Damn, she was a cute kid, just like her mother had been.

A breath hissed out of her with an offended whisper. "Clayton!"

He didn't care that she was a single mother. Despite her accusation, he didn't judge anyone. But he really wanted to know *why* she was a single mother. Had she decided to raise her daughter alone or hadn't she had a choice? Had she turned down the father's offer of marriage, turned off the idea from the poor example her parents had set for her? Or had the guy taken off on her? "Why aren't you married, Abby?"

She snorted. "I should have known you were just acting back at the airport, when you were being nice to Lara. You're still a judgmental jerk."

Instead of anger, amusement coursed through him. She remained a combination of sass and attitude. He could see her turning down marriage, determined to maintain her independence. He persisted. "Why aren't you married?"

"None of your damned business, Clayton."

She was right. Her life was none of his business, but he wanted to know about Lara's father. He could imagine the kind of guys Abby dated:

wild, irresponsible, exciting. His guts twisted into knots at the thought of Abby in some other guy's arms, in some other guy's bed, naked…

He tapped the brakes on his thoughts and the SUV slowed almost to a stop at the entrance to Cloverville Park. "Look there, Abby. Not everything's changed. They still haven't managed to fix the colonel."

Her head turned to where the bronze statue of the town founder, Civil War hero Colonel Clover, stood among the ornamental trees and flowers. His hat was dented, his left ear mangled, his neck at an odd angle with a crude welding job only just holding his head in place, as well as his arms and legs. Her breath hissed out again. "Can't the damn town hire someone to fix him properly? It's been eight years."

Eight years since she'd been expelled from high school for vandalizing the town park by plowing her car across it and knocking over Colonel Clover. She'd been lucky to come out of the crash without even a scratch. His younger sister, Colleen, who'd been in the car, too, *had* been hurt however. Her face had been cut by the broken windshield and her ribs bruised.

The harsh words he'd said to Abby that night rolled through his mind. "Troublemaker" had been the nicest thing he'd called her. God, if

Colleen had been hurt any worse… With his father dying, his family hadn't been able to handle any more tragedy.

He glanced to the backseat, to the little girl who was dependent on Abby alone. *Poor kid.* That was what his father had called Abby, when he'd told Clayton to go easy on her, to give her a chance since she was a remarkable young lady. That was one of the last things his father had ever said to him, because he'd died just a few days later.

Clayton blinked. He should have listened to his dad and been easier on her then. She'd only been a kid. Now, sitting next to him, staring wide-eyed at the park, she didn't look a lot older despite the eight years that had passed and motherhood.

"I guess it's true what they say," Abby said, her voice soft. "You can't come home again."

When she turned to him, her blue eyes bright with unshed tears, his guts twisted with regret over how she'd left town, and with anxiety over her return. Although Abby Hamilton had grown up, he had no doubt she would still cause trouble.

For him.

Chapter Two

Abby leaned into the backseat, brushing the tangle of damp curls from Lara's sleeping face before unclasping her safety belt. Strong hands gripped Abby's waist, the heat of his palms burning through the thin cotton of her tank top. Her heart jumped. Startled, she lifted her head, smacking it against the roof as he gently tugged her out of the doorway.

"I'll get her," Clayton said, pushing Abby aside.

Some things never changed. She brushed a hand over her scalp, checking for a bump as she glared at him. But he'd already turned away to lift out her daughter, settling her sleeping head against his broad shoulder. Abby's heart shifted again at how right Clayton looked with a child in his arms. *Her child*.

"You're going to hurt yourself lifting her. She's nearly as big as you are," he murmured, staring over Lara's head at Abby. "You never grew."

Maybe not physically. But emotionally she had. She knew better than to ever expect a man such as Clayton to be interested in her. She didn't attract the responsible kind. She only attracted the ones who wanted to use her, not love her. But then, maybe the men weren't the problem. If her parents were any indication, she was simply unlovable.

"Abby!" a voice squealed as a group of women rushed off the wide front porch of the Kellys' Victorian. The yellow structure, with its brightly painted teal-and-purple trim, resembled the gingerbread houses the Kelly family baked for their customers every Christmas.

The trio of women enveloped Abby, their voices raised with excitement. She'd always had that effect on Brenna Kelly and Clayton's two sisters. Molly and Colleen had been studious and mature beyond their years until Abby had arrived on the scene with her boundless energy and enthusiasm. While Clayton had worried about her influence on his siblings, his father had said they needed her to lift their spirits and show them how to have fun. Dad had even gone so far as to suggest that Clayton could benefit from her company, too. But Clayton didn't need any more responsibilities.

Roused by the babble of voices, Lara opened her eyes, blinking her long, thick lashes before gazing blearily up at Clayton. He tensed, expecting a fearful outburst of tears. After all, he was a stranger, and the little girl had been shy back at the airport. But her rosebud lips formed themselves into a smile, and she settled against his shoulder with a contented sigh. His heart clenched, as if someone had just wrapped a small hand around it.

"If Mom gets a load of you like that, you're in trouble," Colleen teased, her brown eyes alight with mischief as she stepped back from the huddle around Abby and stared at him.

"For what?" Abby asked, her brow puckered in confusion as her attention shifted back to Clayton and her daughter.

"For hogging her baby," Molly said, reaching out to run her fingers gently over Lara's head. "Hello, sweetheart," she murmured.

Colleen's mouth lifted in a wide smile. "Mom's been nagging Clayton for grandchildren. If she sees him looking so natural with a child in his arms…"

"I like kids," Clayton assured the women and the little girl who stared up at him again, her blue eyes wide with interest in the conversation. "*Other* people's kids."

"You obviously haven't met Josh's twins yet," Colleen murmured with a weary sigh.

"They're good boys," Brenna said, the redhead jumping to the defense of the groom's children while Molly remained silent, her face pale and unreadable.

Was Abby right? Had Molly accepted this proposal too soon? Clayton needed to get his sister alone for a serious conversation. Since she'd come home from med school just two short weeks ago, he hadn't had many opportunities to talk to her. At the time he'd thought she was simply busy with wedding plans, but now he suspected Molly might have been avoiding him.

She turned, leading the way across the lawn and back toward the front porch. "We've been holding dinner for you," she said over her shoulder as she climbed the wide steps.

"I'm sorry we missed the rehearsal," Abby

apologized to her friends. "I should have taken an earlier flight."

"You couldn't predict the delays at O'Hare," Brenna insisted.

Abby laughed, the musical tinkle raising the hairs on Clayton's arms. "This isn't my first trip," she said, refusing to relinquish responsibility. "I should have factored in the possibilities of *technical* difficulties."

The old man had spoken the truth at the airport. Regret, over misjudging her, knotted Clayton's stomach. She hadn't caused problems on purpose. This time.

"Is the rest of the wedding party here?" Abby asked.

Molly shook her head, tumbling her brown curls around her shoulders. "Eric…left me a voice mail. He can't come."

"Tonight?" Abby sighed. "Well, I'll get to talk to him tomorrow. We can catch up then."

"He's not coming tomorrow, either," Molly said, her voice ragged with emotion.

"Is he okay?" Clayton asked, lost in the conversation as significant looks passed between the four women. He'd never had friends as close as they were. Their mastery of silent communication with mere glances had always frustrated him. He'd felt left out. Despite being only a few years older than most of them, he didn't fit in. He'd never known how to have fun the way they did.

"Eric's okay," Brenna answered. "Can you fill in for him tomorrow and walk Abby down the aisle?"

Abby's breath caught at the idea of walking down an aisle with Clayton. She shook her head, puzzled by the flash of panic she'd felt. She didn't intend to marry anyone, *ever,* and risk a situation like the one her parents had known. "That isn't necessary."

She hoped there wouldn't even be a wedding. From the tight expression leeching the color from Molly's beautiful face, Abby knew she was right—that going through with this wedding would be the only mistake Molly McClintock had ever made. Not counting the tattoo, of course, but Abby had talked her into that. This mistake Abby needed to talk her *out* of.

"You can't walk down the aisle by yourself, when everyone else will have a partner," Brenna insisted. "It wouldn't look right."

Abby was used to not "looking" right. She reminded them, "Clayton has another, more important responsibility. He's giving away the bride."

Judging by the gleam in his dark eyes, she suspected he couldn't wait to carry out that particular role. Maybe he thought Molly's marriage would lessen the family pressure on him to reproduce.

Disappointment tugged at her heart. She'd thought Clayton one of the few selfless people she knew, but she shouldn't be surprised that she'd misjudged a man. She'd done the same with Lara's father, thinking him a man she could trust, and being proven wrong.

With a steady job and a serious demeanor, he'd reminded her of Clayton. Unlike the oldest McClintock sibling, Jeff had refused to take on any responsibility. He'd even refused to believe that Lara was his and that the contraceptive had failed. But Abby wasn't like her mother. She didn't sleep around, and she'd actually thought she'd loved him until he let her down—like everyone else. She didn't know which of them was the bigger fool—Jeff for failing her and Lara, or Abby for trusting him in the first place.

"Clayton can walk down the aisle with you *and* give away the bride," Mrs. McClintock said, as if she'd been listening all along, rather than jumping into the conversation as the group joined her in the kitchen of the Kelly house.

"So how was your trip, honey?" she asked Abby, setting down a bowl of salad and enveloping her in a hug.

Abby stretched her arms around Mrs. McClintock's back, holding tight to the older woman's softness and warmth. The mingled scents of vanilla and cinnamon clung to the woman's shoulder-length brown hair. She probably dyed it now, as she had not even a strand of gray, and this woman had earned more gray hairs than anyone Abby knew. She'd survived the loss of her beloved husband and the raising of four headstrong children. Abby's heart stretched with admiration and love for the woman she'd always wished had been her mother, too.

Nearly choked with emotion, Abby managed to say, "The flight was fine."

And the flight, although late, had been fine. The ride to Cloverville, thanks to Clayton, had not. At least he'd answered the question she'd carried with her for the past eight years. He would never let her forget about the screwed-up girl she'd once been. In his eyes, at least, she would always be the legendary troublemaker from Cloverville.

Mrs. McClintock released Abby, to reach for Lara and take the drowsy child from Clayton's arms. "Oh, she's gotten so big since the last time I was in Chicago. She looks more and more like you every time I see her."

Every time she saw her. Molly wasn't the only family member Clayton intended to get alone for a conversation. Why had his mother never told him about Abby's daughter?

More importantly, why did his arms feel so empty right now without Lara? He drew in a deep breath, catching a whiff of grilling beef through the open patio doors. Mr. Kelly was as renowned for his barbecuing as his baking, but Clayton's hunger barely stirred. Abby Hamilton had been back in town for little more than an hour and already he'd lost his appetite.

He glanced over at her, grudgingly appreciative of how her curves filled out the white tank top and tight jeans. Her friends were all in casual dresses because of the rehearsal, but here she was, still dressed like a teenager. A damned sexy one, he had to acknowledge. Apparently he'd only lost his appetite for food.

But more than her body drew his interest. Her face softened with affection as she gazed at his mom and her daughter. Her expression of love touched something deep in his chest, bringing about another kind of longing—one he had no business feeling.

"Clayton, where's Erin?" his mother asked.

"Erin?" he repeated, distracted.

"She means Ellen," Colleen said. Even outside the agency, she sometimes acted like her brother's office manager. "Weren't you bringing her tonight?"

"She couldn't make it."

"A lot of people couldn't make it tonight," Brenna noted, as she picked up tongs to finish tossing the salad greens. The maid of honor's voice deepened with frustration when she added, "Even the best man didn't show up. It's going to be pure chaos tomorrow."

Despite her friend's concern, Abby smiled. They had always considered Brenna the mother of the group. She liked being in control almost as much as Clayton did, which was why she'd already taken over and expanded her parents' bakery. Abby had occasionally wondered why Clayton had never gotten together with the voluptuous redhead, since they had so much in common. But he'd always treated Brenna simply as if she were one of his sisters. Maybe it was because she shared the same Irish and Italian heritage the McClintocks had. Or maybe it was because Clayton had approved of Brenna, whereas he'd never approved of Abby.

Eight years had passed, and she didn't seek his approval anymore—his or anyone else's in Cloverville. She'd only come back for Molly's wedding. The bride-to-be slid her arm around Abby's waist. "So you're not the only one who won't know what she's doing tomorrow," Molly teased.

Abby bit her tongue, holding back her comments about Molly not knowing what she was doing, either. Along with learning how to manage her ADD, she'd acquired some tact over the years. If only she could remember those lessons around Clayton....

But he distracted her. "I'm going to join the guys outside," he said as he stepped through the open doorway, obviously anxious to escape her presence.

Lara, however, wasn't eager to let him go. She wriggled out of Mrs. McClintock's arms. "Can I go, too, Mommy?" she asked. When Abby reluctantly offered a nod, the child ran out after him, reaching for Clayton's hand as two boys about her age ran up to them. They were dark-haired, blue-eyed miniatures of the man who stood beside Mr. Kelly at the grill. But Lara was obviously not charmed by their cuteness, and she clung to Clayton until the twins ran off across the backyard.

"Clayton has a fan," his mother said, grinning as she picked up the salad bowl and joined the others on the patio, leaving Molly, Brenna, Colleen and Abby alone in the kitchen.

A wide smile spread across Colleen's face. "This is so great. We're all here together again."

"Except for one of us." Molly reminded her younger sister of Eric's absence.

Abby had a pretty good idea about why Eric had backed out of being a groomsman. She imagined he would still probably rather be Molly's groom. Apparently a lot of things hadn't changed.

"It's so great to have you home, Abby," Colleen exclaimed, throwing her arms around Abby's neck.

Despite her concern over the impending marriage, Abby's heart swelled with happiness. She patted Colleen's back. "Hey, it's not like you guys haven't seen me in years. You've visited me. Not often enough," she playfully observed, "but at least you've visited."

"It's not the same as having you here," Colleen insisted. "Now that you've given up your place in Chicago, you need to move back to Cloverville. You can open the third branch of Temps to Go here."

The request wasn't exactly new. Abby had fielded it repeatedly in phone calls, letters and e-mails. She'd never been able to make Colleen understand that, to her, Cloverville could *never* be home. So instead of arguing, she changed the subject. "Brenna, did you hire any strippers for tonight?"

Colleen's thin body shook with laughter. With her graceful build and gorgeous face, the girl could have been a supermodel rather than an office manager. But like her big brother, she might have assumed her career out of a sense of obligation. Or guilt—as Abby well knew.

Regret dimmed Abby's happiness as she considered the part she'd played in Colleen's guilt. Maybe Clayton was right. Maybe she had caused too much trouble in the McClintock household.

"Strippers?" Colleen shook her head. "You haven't met the groom yet. No stripper could measure up to him."

"We're not having strippers," Brenna insisted, her expression strained. Not that she would disapprove of strippers—Brenna Kelly was no prude. Was she stressed with her responsibilities as maid of honor? From the long-distance conversations she'd had over the past few weeks, Abby suspected Brenna had more interest in planning the wedding than the bride had. And maybe more interest in the groom.

"It looks like dinner's ready," the redhead murmured as she stepped outside to join the others on the patio.

"Come on," Colleen pleaded with her sister. "You can share Josh with us for one night. You're going to have him for the rest of your life."

What little color there had been in Molly's face drained away, leaving her skin almost translucent.

"The thought of spending the rest of my life with one particular someone would give me the willies, too," Abby admitted. Not that anyone would want her forever. Even her own parents hadn't wanted her.

Molly shook her head. "No, it's just that…"

"What?" Abby persisted, hoping Molly would finally admit to her doubts.

But the brunette laughed. "*I* haven't even seen him naked yet."

Colleen sighed. "What a waste. But at least

Clayton will be happy you saved yourself for marriage."

Abby suspected that her friend had waited to make love to Josh for a reason other than her big brother's approval. Molly didn't love her groom. And if she couldn't sleep with him, she certainly couldn't marry him.

Molly's dark eyes welled with tears, summoning every protective instinct Clayton possessed. What had Abby said to her? They'd only been alone together in the house for a few moments.

He asked his brother, Rory, to entertain Lara and went over to Molly. "Honey, are you okay?" he asked, using the same tone he had with Lara. His sister seemed as vulnerable and afraid as Abby's daughter had when she'd met him at the airport. Yet Molly had always been the strongest of his three siblings.

What had Abby said to her? He turned his attention from his sister to the blond troublemaker, and although she never slowed her conversation with his mother and Mrs. Kelly, Abby met his stare and then closed one eye in an audacious wink.

Molly laughed, even as the tears shimmered on her lashes. "Nothing much has changed between the two of you," she commented.

"What do you mean?" There had never been anything between the two of them but animosity.

"You can't keep your eyes off each other."

Clayton's pulse quickened. Did Abby watch him in the way that he watched her? "I'm just making sure she's not starting trouble again."

"Isn't that excuse getting old, Clayton?"

Maybe it was. But he wasn't about to admit his attraction to Abby, not even to himself. Nothing could come of it. Abby hadn't been able to wait to leave Cloverville, and there was no way she was staying now. And even if she did, he wasn't interested.

"Look at you, Mol. You're crying. She's only been back a little while and she upset you."

"These aren't those kind of tears," Molly insisted.

"You're happy?"

Her gaze slid away from his. "I'm happy Abby's back home, where she belongs. I hope she stays."

Clayton's stomach dropped. He hoped she didn't. He didn't know how long he could deny the attraction. "Are you happy about tomorrow?" he asked. "About getting married?"

Molly gestured, hand shaking, toward where the groom-to-be stood near the grill, a twin on each arm, like matching blue-eyed, dark-haired bookends. "He's a great guy. Successful, handsome, generous and a wonderful father."

But did she love him? Hell, what did Clayton know about love? Only that it could hurt so much he didn't intend to learn any more about it than he already knew. He'd seen his mother's devastation when his father died, and he didn't intend to risk that kind of pain himself. It was better to feel *nothing,* he was certain.

"So you're sure…?" he asked his sister. "You're doing what *you* want to do?"

Even as she nodded, more tears pooled in her eyes. Her voice broke when she answered, "Yes."

Clayton pulled her into a hug. "I'm honored to be giving you away tomorrow, but I wish…"

It didn't matter what he wished. Nothing could bring back his father.

"I know," Molly said, pressing her lips to Clayton's cheek before pulling from his arms. "Me, too. But you'll do, big brother. I can't thank you enough for everything you've done for us. For paying for my college and med school."

"*I* didn't," he protested. "It's really Dad's…"

"It's *your* money," she corrected. "You're the one working your butt off at the office. He's been gone eight years, Clayton. It's *your* office. *Your* agency. *Your* money. I can't believe you even insisted on paying for the wedding. Josh wanted to pay."

"Dad would have wanted…" He suppressed the emotion that was threatening to choke him. "It's the right thing to do."

"And Clayton always does the right thing," she teased him.

What about her? Did she really feel getting married tomorrow was the right thing? "Molly…"

She kissed his cheek again, and one of her tears dropped onto his neck. "Thank you."

He reached out, but she turned and ran back into the house. Before he could follow her, a soft hand slid over his forearm, pulling him up short.

His pulse didn't jump, so it couldn't be *her.* Instead of Abby, his mother tugged on his arm. "Come to the buffet and get some food, Clayton, before your brother eats it all. The way that kid eats, he must have a tapeworm."

"Mom, I should check on Molly."

"She's okay," she insisted. "All brides get emotional."

He hoped that was all it was and that nothing else was going on with his sister. Of all his siblings, he'd worried the least about Molly. She'd always been so focused, so determined to achieve her goals. Ever since their father died, she'd wanted to be a doctor. Getting married was a little detour from finishing med school and her residency, but he had no doubt she would still achieve her goals.

Unless…

Abby had referred to the ceremony as a shotgun wedding. Could Molly be pregnant? Did she *have* to get married? He wouldn't have thought so. The groom had been so traditional that he'd even asked Clayton for Molly's hand in marriage. But nowadays that really didn't mean anything. He allowed himself a selfish moment of satisfaction. Maybe Mom would soon have more than enough grandchildren to keep her happy and off his back.

"How come no one told me about Lara?" he asked her. The question had been burning in his mind since the airport.

His mother smiled her softening-the-blow

smile. He'd seen it often over the years. "You tend to be judgmental, honey."

First Abby. Now his own mother. Stung, he clenched his jaw. "I am not judgmental of people."

"Oh, not *people,*" she agreed. "Just Abby. That's why she made us promise not to tell you."

So Abby had wanted to keep her daughter secret from him. Why? He'd never considered the fact that she might care about what he thought of her.

"Speaking of Abby," his mother continued, "you need to drop her back at the house. Instead of a bachelorette party, the girls are having one of their infamous sleepovers at our house. Then we'll all leave together for the church in the morning."

He winced at the memory of those adolescent sleepovers. They hadn't bothered him much when they were all younger, except for the incessant giggling that had kept him awake half the night. But he'd really hated it when they'd had them years later, on his weekends home from college. Abby had run around the house in skimpy boy shorts and a tank top. His wince turned into a groan that he smothered with a cough.

"I'll switch her bags to your car," he offered.

She shook her head. "Nonsense. That's too much trouble."

For whom?

"And Rory needs to spend the night at your place."

"The best man was supposed to use my spare bedroom." Despite all the recent construction, Cloverville still had no hotels or motels.

"He's coming straight to the church in the morning, and so the groom doesn't see the bride before the wedding, Josh and the boys are staying here at the Kellys'. You have room for Rory tonight."

Room, maybe, but he wasn't so sure he had the patience, especially not after seeing Abby again. He'd have to stay awake all night to guard his liquor cabinet. Clayton focused his gaze on Mr. Kelly's cooler, beside which his curly-haired teenage brother stood—probably about ready to snitch a beer. Clayton had caught him with a bottle a few weeks ago, in the park, well after his curfew. The boy was trying to grow up too fast and too recklessly. Fortunately, the old man who'd seen Rory and his friends while walking his dog had called

Clayton instead of the sheriff or their mother. That time, too, he'd had to leave his date in order to rescue Rory from himself.

It wouldn't matter if both Molly and Colleen got married. He'd *still* have too much on his hands with Rory to consider getting seriously involved with anyone. But he wouldn't change his mind about a relationship even if Rory suddenly became a choirboy.

Abby sauntered up next to Rory, whose face flushed red. Clayton's gaze followed his brother's to her derriere, straining the worn seams of her jeans as she leaned over the cooler, drew out a can and handed it to the boy. A cola.

Amusement teased his lips into a grin. His mother patted his cheek. "It's great to see you smile, Clayton. You're always so serious. Too serious. You need something…" Her gaze followed his to the giggling blonde teasing his brother. "Or *someone* to lighten you up."

It didn't matter how many grandchildren Molly gave her, he wasn't likely to get his mother off his back. Ever. Because he wasn't going to get married and start a family with anyone. And most especially not with Abby Hamilton.

Chapter Three

"So are you my chauffeur for as long as I'm here?" Abby asked as Clayton pulled into his mother's driveway behind Mrs. McClintock's minivan. She'd beat them home, with Lara in the back in the built-in car seat. Abby had wanted to ride with them, but Mrs. McClintock had insisted there wasn't room with Colleen, Molly and Rory, who'd had to come home to pack his bag for Clayton's.

He lived in town in the apartment above the insurance agency. Abby couldn't imagine willingly leaving this home. Her heart lifted at the sight of the Dutch colonial where she'd spent so much time in her younger days.

Although she suspected Rory had long out-
grown it, the tire still swung from the giant
oak in the front yard. The house wasn't as
colorful or as big as the Kellys' Victorian,
but Abby preferred its white siding and black
roof. To her, it represented all the stability
she'd never had in her own family. This house
was why she'd packed up her apartment in
Chicago. She wanted to raise her daughter
in a house just like this.

Too bad it was in Cloverville.

"Mrs. Hild's roses and Mr. Carpenter's
storefront thank you for not driving." He
turned toward her, his eyes gleaming in
the dim glow of the dashboard lights, as he
added, "Not to mention the colonel."

"Not to mention, and yet you did. You just
can't let it go. We're both adults now. Why
can't you put the past behind us?" she asked.

Why was he so determined to think the
worst of her?

"I'm just teasing you," he claimed.

"I'm not one of your sisters, Clayton."

His gaze clung to hers as he leaned over
the console, his face so close that his breath
brushed her face when he whispered, "I know."

Abby shivered, her attention drawn to his
lips. But then he pulled back and opened his

door. Her breath shuddered out, and when she reached for her door latch, her hand shook. Had he been about to kiss her? Clayton McClintock kiss her? She hated to admit it, even to herself, but growing up she had daydreamed about his kisses, how they'd make her feel…

Wanted. She shook her head, pushing aside the old longing, which she knew would never be fulfilled. Clayton's kisses or anyone wanting her for keeps.

"I'm sorry you had to drive out of your way for me," she said, surprised he'd come around to her side of the vehicle, as if he'd been about to open her door.

Clayton McClintock opening her door? Clayton McClintock teasing her? Perhaps she wasn't the only one who'd changed.

"I have to pick up Rory, anyway," he said as he headed around the SUV to unlatch the back door.

"But he could have ridden home with you, instead of your coming out here." Her face flushed as she realized who had maneuvered the passenger lists. "Your mother…"

"She's not exactly being subtle," he said, with a short, bitter laugh. "She thinks you'd be good for me. That you'd lighten me up."

Abby snorted. Mrs. Mick playing matchmaker for her and *Clayton?*

"Exactly," he agreed with her snort of derision. Too quickly. Obviously he had no interest in her, despite his teasing. "She doesn't understand. You've always brought out the worst in me."

If she'd only seen his worst, what was Clayton's best?

"How long are you staying here?" he asked as he hefted her bags from the back. She'd certainly packed more than a couple days' worth of clothes. But then she had a daughter, and he had no idea how much stuff one needed with little kids. And he never intended to find out. He was still raising one family, and he had no intention of raising another.

A mocking smile tugged at her lips. "Don't worry, Clayton. I'm not going to be here long enough for your mother to get us to the altar."

He refused to take her bait. She was much better at teasing than he was, despite his having three younger siblings. Instead, he carried her bags to the door. "The only wedding I'm worried about is the one that's taking place tomorrow."

"That *may* be taking place tomorrow," she replied.

He dropped the bags on the cement stoop in front of the door and turned back, trapping her between his body and the side of his mother's minivan. "You're *not* going to talk Molly out of getting married."

Molly might have been emotional, but she'd seemed so sure that she wanted to marry Dr. Josh Towers. She didn't need anyone making her doubt her decision.

Abby's lips lifted in that infuriating smile she kept flashing him. He longed to wipe it off her mouth—with his. Breathing deep, he calmed his rising temper. No one, not even Rory, tested his control the way Abby did.

"What kind of friend would that make me?" she asked him.

"Talking her out of getting married?" He knew that she wouldn't purposely do anything to hurt her friends. "You might think that makes you a good friend."

She nodded. "I might."

"But you wouldn't be a good friend if you're actually projecting your aversion to marriage onto her," he observed. "Just because you think marriage isn't for you, that doesn't mean that it isn't for Molly."

"If you're so pro-marriage, why isn't there a ring on *your* finger?" she asked, reaching for his hand. Her skin brushed against his as she stroked his bare ring finger.

The hair rose on Clayton's forearms—her touch was like an electrical charge. He pulled his hand away. "I've never been in love."

And he damn well never intended to fall prey to that dangerous emotion.

"What makes you think Molly is?" she persisted.

He wasn't certain Molly was in love. Yet. But she respected Josh and she'd chosen to spend her life with him. It wasn't up to Clayton or Abby to change her mind.

"She's wearing a ring," he reminded her. "She *accepted* his proposal."

"But I don't think she loves him."

He swallowed hard, but he couldn't control his curiosity about her and about Lara's father any longer. "Have *you* ever been in love, Abby?"

She shook her head, tumbling blond curls around her bare shoulders.

"But you have a daughter…"

Her laugh trilled out. "Clayton, you're so old-fashioned."

Yeah, maybe he was.

"And judgmental," she accused him again. "I could have become a nun instead of a single mother, and you still wouldn't approve of me."

"Is that why you made everyone promise *not* to tell me about Lara?" he asked, stepping so close their bodies nearly touched. "You were worried about what I'd think of you?"

She lifted her chin and tossed her head with all the spirit of a champion racehorse. "I don't care what you think of me, Clayton."

Anger licked through him, heating his blood. She didn't care what he thought? It shouldn't bother him, but it did. "Then why didn't you want anyone to tell me?" he persisted. "Are you ashamed you made a mistake?"

He stumbled back, nearly tripping over her luggage, as her hands slammed into his chest.

"*Never* call her that!" Her voice trembled with rage. "Never call my daughter a mistake."

He caught her by the shoulders, holding her gently but firmly so she'd stop pushing him. "I'm *sorry,* Abby." She definitely brought out the worst in him. "That wasn't what I meant."

He could never see a child, any child, as a mistake. And even before Abby had reacted so strongly, he'd known she didn't see her daughter that way, either. She *loved* Lara.

Instead of defending himself, he conceded, "I was out of line."

"Yes, you were," she agreed, drawing in a deep breath. Her eyes pooled with unshed tears.

"I better go," he said, releasing her to open the door to the kitchen of his old house. His hand shook, rattling the handle.

"Clayton?"

He turned back to her.

"Don't worry," she said. "I'm leaving Cloverville right after the wedding."

He nodded, relief easing some of the tension that pressed against his chest. No matter what his mother, the matchmaker, thought, they weren't good for each other.

"I'll see you tomorrow, then," he said, setting her suitcases inside the door. "At the church."

"Yeah, at the church…"

Unless she talked Molly out of going through with the marriage, which was her intention. She passed through the kitchen doorway, her back nearly grazing his chest. She suppressed another shiver, due no doubt to the cool night air. And not to Clayton's proximity, nor the memory of the way the muscles in his arms and shoulders had rippled as he'd carried her bags.

"Hey, man," Rory said from where he leaned against the center island. "What took you so long? They're having a *slumber* party." He rolled his eyes, trying to act macho either to impress his older brother or just because he was a teenage boy.

"Wait for me in the car, then," Clayton suggested. "I'll just bring these bags upstairs."

"That's not necessary," Abby protested as she followed him up the back stairs to the second story. Why did he have to act macho, too? Was that a brother thing? "I can carry my own bags. They've kicked Rory out. You're not supposed to be up here, you know."

"My eyes are closed," he insisted, in deference to the pajama party. "What room did Mom give you?"

When she said nothing, he opened his eyes again, his gaze meeting hers. "Mine. Of course." He dumped his bags inside the open door.

"It's not your room anymore," she reminded him, but she followed his gaze toward the bed she'd be sleeping in. *His* bed. A shiver raised bumps on her bare arms. She had to remind herself that she was still mad at him for calling Lara a mistake. Honesty forced her to admit that he really hadn't called her daughter that; he'd figured that was Abby's reason for keeping her secret. Shame. But the only shame she felt was over her attraction to a man who would always think the worst of her.

"Abby, I'm really…"

She didn't want another apology. She just wanted him gone. "Go, get out of here." She gestured toward the stairs. "Girls only!"

"He probably wanted to hang around to catch a glimpse of you in your pj's," Colleen teased, leaning out her bedroom doorway as Clayton tromped down the steps. "He has always stared at you."

"He was just trying to intimidate me into going home." Never mind that the McClintocks' house had always felt more like home than the rented bungalow she'd shared with her mother while her father spent most of his time away, driving a semi. But her mother actually hadn't spent much of her time at their run-down place, either. She'd mostly been in the bar.

"So where's Brenna?" she asked as she joined the two sisters in their old bedroom. Even though Clayton's room was empty, Colleen and Molly still doubled up when Molly came home from school. Abby envied the closeness between them. Growing up, she had wanted a sister desperately, and so she'd made the McClintock girls into hers.

"Brenna stayed behind to help her mother clean up," Molly explained as she painted her nails on top of some newspapers spread across the comforter. "And she didn't want to leave her parents alone with T.J. and Buzz."

Buzz was undoubtedly the twin whose dark hair had been "buzz" cut much shorter than his brother's. Abby suspected he'd borrowed his father's electric razor.

"Why? They were managing fine." Abby recalled Mr. and Mrs. Kelly's smiling faces and easy laughter as they'd played with the boys. Clayton probably wasn't the only one under parental pressure to provide grandchildren.

"Maybe *too* fine," Colleen agreed. "Mom might have to fight them for rights as a grandparent."

"That's just like Brenna to choose responsibility over fun," Abby observed. "She and Clayton would be a perfect match." So why wasn't his mother trying to set up the two of them? Why was she playing matchmaker with Abby, who didn't even intend to stay in town? To keep her and Lara in Cloverville? Mrs. Mick was the only "grandparent" Lara had ever known.

"Clayton's never looked at Brenna the way he looks at you," Colleen teased her. She *had* to be teasing.

"We're not going to stay up all night talking about Clayton," Abby insisted, determined to change the subject.

"So this isn't going to be like our old slumber parties, then." Molly laughed.

"We never stayed up all night talking about Clayton."

"*We* never did," Colleen agreed. "But you did."

Obviously, her two friends had joined forces with their matchmaking mother. And they were making things up. The only reason Abby would have talked about Clayton at all back then would have been to complain about how he spoiled their fun. She picked up a pillow and chucked it at Colleen's head.

"Mommy! You're not supposed to throw things in the house," Lara chastised her as she and Mrs. McClintock stood in the doorway.

The older woman's face was illuminated with contentment. "It's so great to have my girls home again," she mused. "I'll read Lara a story and tuck her into bed. You go back to gossiping about boys, like you used to."

Abby kissed her daughter on the forehead. "Hey, sweetheart, thank you for being so good today." She'd been extremely patient waiting for their flight—more patient, Abby suspected, then Clayton had been.

"I'm always good, Mommy," Lara reminded her matter-of-factly. She waved at Molly and Colleen as Mrs. McClintock carried her off to bed.

"Are you sure she's yours?" Molly teased. "She's so sweet."

Abby occasionally wondered herself. "You were there when I had her," she observed. "Well, at least you were there until you passed out."

Abby's best friends had come to Detroit for Lara's birth. Mrs. Mick had come along, too. Without their support, she didn't know what she would have done. She'd been terrified.

"A doctor who passes out at the sight of blood..." Colleen began.

"Hey, I was exhausted," Molly said defensively. "I can barely fit sleep into my schedule."

But she'd always fit her friends into it. Because she'd been there for Abby, Abby had to be here for Molly, coming back to Cloverville and saying what needed to be said.

"Lara's a good girl," Abby said, "but kids are a lot of responsibility."

"Oh, my God. Clayton's already gotten to her. She's talking about responsibility." Colleen shook her head, sending waves of satiny brown hair shimmering around her shoulders.

"Kids deserve responsible parents, that's all." Not selfish ones like hers had been. "They deserve stability and love. Mol, you know I love you, but if you're having any doubts—and I think you are—you shouldn't get married tomorrow. It's not fair to the boys or to Josh."

Before she'd met Josh, Abby had figured her friend had accepted his proposal out of pity because he'd been raising his sons alone since their mother abandoned them when they were babies.

Molly's husband-to-be seemed like a nice guy—and as gorgeous as Colleen had mentioned. Abby could understand why a woman would accept his proposal. For anything.

"But most of all, honey," Abby said, settling onto the bed and looping an arm around Molly's shoulders, "it's not fair to *you*."

"The wedding is tomorrow," Molly replied, her voice heavy with misery, as she laid her head on Abby's shoulder.

Abby's stomach tightened. Her friend *was* having doubts. "Until you say, 'I do,' it's not too late to back out."

"Clayton will kill me."

Abby laughed, knowing exactly on whom he'd lay the blame for a canceled wedding. "No, he won't. He'll kill *me*."

Abby cracked open the door and peered across an empty vestibule into the church. Bunches of lilies and carnations adorned each pew. Sunlight shone through stained-glass windows behind the altar, casting the entire church in a rainbow of colors.

"Is anybody here yet?" Brenna asked from the anteroom, where she sat with Lara, Colleen and the bride.

Abby ducked back as she caught sight of several early arrivals. An older lady wearing a wide-brimmed hat and a wildly flowered dress particularly caught her attention. "Mrs. Hild."

"She's the organist for the ceremony."

"Great. Just great." The older woman would probably be about as happy to see Abby as

Clayton had been. Cautiously she eased the door open farther, looking toward the other end of the hall and the groom's room. As she watched, someone stepped out—Clayton Mc-Clintock in a black tux with a pleated shirt, the white fabric crisp and complementary to his tanned skin and brown hair and eyes. A sigh slipped from between her lips. *Damn.*

When he turned toward her, she shut the door and shakily leaned back against the frame. She didn't belong here. Not in this church, and most definitely not in Cloverville. Every one of the town's busybodies would be able to nod her head in confirmation of the old claims that she was, indeed, her mother's daughter. Sure, Abby's parents had been married...two months after her birth. And then, in those pre-paternity test days, her father had often claimed she wasn't really his child. Abby suspected that even her mother hadn't known for sure.

No, Abby *wasn't* her mother's daughter. Her bad driving hadn't been the result of drinking, as the townspeople might have thought, but of her ADD. And furthermore, Abby knew who Lara's father was—she only wished he'd been someone else, someone who'd have wanted both her and their baby.

"You okay, Mommy?" Lara asked, sitting

perfectly still while Brenna wove flowers into her hair.

Abby couldn't sit that quietly even now. If not for the fact that Lara looked so much like her, she might well have thought they'd switched her baby with someone else's at the hospital. The child deserved more than Abby could give her—a stable home, a loving family. All she had was Abby.

But she worked hard to give her daughter everything she needed, and to be the kind of mother her daughter deserved. She blinked to clear her eyes as she gazed at Lara. "Oh, baby, you're just so beautiful."

"You're beautiful, too, Mommy."

Brenna whistled. "You really are. What a gorgeous bridesmaid's dress. Someone with fabulous taste picked out these dresses."

Abby glanced down at the strapless red satin gown. "Oh, I don't know. I think they're kind of tacky."

Brenna tossed a red carnation at her.

"Hey!" Abby protested, dodging the delicate blossom. "You're setting a bad example."

"You'd know about that," a male voice, deep with amusement, said from beyond the door. Clayton teasing her again?

Her heart thudded against her ribs.

"Who's that?" Lara asked in a shy whisper. "Is it Rory?" Last night, at the Kellys', she'd fallen a little in love with the teenager who'd quite sweetly played with her more than Josh's rambunctious twins had been willing to. Rory, with his curly mop of hair and huge brown eyes, was hard to resist. Abby, herself, had fallen for him years ago, when he was a grinning, toothless baby. She'd helped his sisters babysit him. He had only been a couple of years older than Lara was now when Abby had left Cloverville, but it seemed to her he'd grown up so fast.

"No, it's not Rory," Abby told her.

"Clayton," Colleen said, even though she was actually too far from the door to have heard his voice. She'd simply read Abby's face instead. She sat at the vanity, touching up her makeup. Molly sat beside her sister, staring blindly into the mirror.

"You okay, Mol?" Abby asked, just as she had earlier, but this time with more than a twinge of guilt. Maybe she'd been too vocal last night, on the subject of Molly marrying a virtual stranger. One who came with two kids. If Molly had any doubts, she and the groom wouldn't be the only ones hurt—the kids would be, too. And they didn't deserve that. They deserved someone who would love them completely.

Going by the few dates she'd had since Lara was born, Abby knew that it wasn't easy finding someone who could love your child as you did. Heck, she'd never been able to find anyone who could even love *her.* Abby. Except for her friends and Mrs. Mick.

The door rattled behind her, and Clayton spoke. "Everybody decent? Let me in."

Abby braced her body against it. "Molly?"

"I'm fine."

"You're not even dressed yet," Brenna said, gesturing toward a confection of white satin and lace that hung from a special hook on the wall. Molly sat at the vanity in faded jeans, a zip-up gray sweatshirt and her headpiece. "Let us help you," she insisted.

Molly shook her head, setting ringlets atremble against her veil. "I can manage. It's just one zipper." She'd always been so independent, so determined. "I really need a minute alone. Can all of you step outside?"

"Molly…" Brenna protested.

"Please," she implored them, using her expressive eyes to bring home the request to give her a little space.

Abby sighed. She'd spoken her mind, and

her friend knew how she felt about this wedding. Maybe Molly needed a minute alone now to figure out how *she* felt about it. "Okay, gals, let's give her a little space." She straightened up and stepped away from the door, opening it to Clayton's concerned gaze.

"It's almost time," he said, tapping a finger on his gold watch. "Molly, you aren't even dressed."

Abby pressed her hands against his chest and pushed, but not as she had the night before. Today, she could appreciate the ripple of muscle beneath her palms, the warmth that penetrated his crisp shirt. She swallowed hard, then said calmly but firmly, "Back off. The bride needs a minute."

"Molly?" He spoke over Abby's head, ignoring her words and her restraint, his voice full of concern for his sister. "Are you all right?"

While Abby respected the fact that Clayton cared for his siblings, Molly didn't need any pressure from anyone right now. Her fingers pressed into the pleats of his shirt and she pushed once more. "Give her some space."

His heart leapt, beating fast against her hand. He stared down at her, his voice a warning as he uttered her name. "Abby..."

She shivered, wishing her dress wasn't strapless. His gaze skimmed over her shoulders to where the tight bodice pushed up more cleavage than she'd realized she had. His dark eyes flared.

Brenna pushed past them. "Come on, the bride wants some time alone." She dropped her voice lower as she led Lara out. "I'm not sure what you two want."

Neither did Clayton. Although she didn't say anything, Colleen sent her brother an arched stare as she filed out behind Brenna and Lara. When Abby moved to pass him, he caught her by the wrist, wrapping his fingers around the delicate bones. She was so small.

"I want to talk to you," he said, closing the door to give the bride the privacy she'd requested.

He couldn't blame Molly. She was about to take on some major responsibilities: a husband and two boisterous young boys. He couldn't imagine willingly putting himself in her position. But she'd made her decision, and once Molly made up her mind, she stuck to it. Unless someone who'd proven to be a bad influence in the past had managed to sway her. But Molly was at the church, about to put on her dress and about to walk down the aisle. Molly was fine, he assured himself.

Gently he tugged on Abby's wrist, leading her into an alcove off the vestibule. "I want to apologize for last night."

He couldn't believe he'd suggested that Lara was a mistake. His words had kept him awake all last night, plagued with guilt.

"Don't," she said, shaking her wrist to lose his grasp.

He held fast, however, his fingers stroking her soft skin, registering her leaping pulse. "Don't what?" he asked, his own heart racing.

"Don't be nice, Clayton." Her blue eyes, wide with apprehension, stared up at him. "We're not nice to each other."

He sighed. "That was then. I shouldn't have been so hard on you," he admitted. "You were just a kid."

"Were *you* ever just a kid, Clayton?" she asked, and her voice lowered to a whisper. "Haven't you ever done anything you regretted?"

God, she reached deep inside him, pulling out thoughts he hadn't considered in so long—the past, with all his youthful dreams and fantasies. He'd buried the lot of them with his father. Still he had no regrets. "Not yet

I haven't." Although if she stuck around, if she kept tempting him, he might. "Except for what I said to you last night…"

"Forget about it," she replied. And this time when she tugged on her wrist, he released her. "I already have."

She reached up. Her nails, the same deep crimson as her dress, scraped his throat as she adjusted his black bow tie. He drew in a deep breath, reacting instinctively to her touch, her closeness. The scent of lilies drifted up from the single perfect flower nestled in her blond curls. Then her fingers skimmed his chin. "Don't worry, Clayton. I'll be gone soon."

Not soon enough for him, for his peace of mind. Abby stepped out of the alcove, into the throng of arriving guests. Her laugh rang out as she greeted people she hadn't seen in years. She appeared unconcerned, but Clayton knew she was merely acting.

He moved back toward the bride's dressing room, and when he raised his hand to knock, he found he was shaking. Yeah, Abby couldn't leave soon enough for him. "Molly?"

"Yes?"

"Are you ready?" he called out.

"Yes. I'm ready," she answered.

"I'll ask Brenna to tell them to start the

music." She was in charge, after all, having far more to do with the arrangements than the bride had had.

Now, Brenna lined up the wedding party. She took her place beside the best man, Dr. Nick Jameson. Colleen and Rory would walk together after Abby and before the flower girl and twin ring bearers, leaving Clayton to walk down with Abby before going back to retrieve the bride.

When Abby's fingers closed around his arm, his muscles tensed. He didn't know exactly what it was about her touch, but he could still feel the pressure of her hand against his thigh from the day before. What would it have felt like directly against his skin?

He closed his eyes and forced himself to breathe. Brenna turned back toward him and said, "You're sure Molly's all right? She wouldn't let us back in to check on her."

He nodded. "She told me she was ready."

"Okay, here we go," Brenna said, and then she and the best man headed down the aisle.

A few beats later, Clayton and Abby followed. Actually, she led. "Who's speeding now?" he murmured, and glanced down at her. Her face pinched and pale, she stared down all those townspeople she'd left behind eight years ago. He couldn't imagine what she must be feeling at the moment. She'd left in disgrace at eighteen, and now she'd returned as a single mother. He honestly didn't judge her for that, but he suspected that some people might in their conservative town.

When they reached the altar, she held his arm for an extra moment before releasing him to step behind Brenna. He hesitated, irrationally feeling as if he'd deserted her. If she needed protection, she had her friends. She didn't need him.

He turned, walked past the groom and best man and then slipped around the last pew to return to the vestibule. Just inside the open doors to the church Lara stood between Buzz and T.J. The boys were tussling over a pillow that would have held the wedding rings, had their father trusted them with them. Lara's tiny fingers clutched a basket of crimson rose petals. With her golden hair and pale skin, she looked angelic in her gown of white lace and satin.

He crouched to her level and asked, "Sweetheart, are you okay?"

She shifted her gaze from the basket of petals, her eyes wide with apprehension, as her mother's had been a minute earlier.

"You're going to be great," Clayton assured her, resting his hand on her shoulder for a quick squeeze before she and the tuxedoed twins started down the aisle. The boys rushed ahead while Lara painstakingly dropped her petals, one at a time, upon the white runner. Gentle laughter rippled through the congregation. From the front of the church, Abby beamed an encouraging smile at her daughter.

Clayton's breath caught and held. Abby had never looked more beautiful to him. But he would have to pull his gaze away. He didn't have time for the feelings that were rushing through him. He didn't have time for the kind of trouble Abby Hamilton would bring to his life.

Reminded of his responsibilities, he headed back to find Molly. Why wasn't she out already? She was taking this no-one-seeing-the-bride-in-her-wedding-gown thing a little too far. "Molly?"

When she didn't answer his knock, he turned the knob and pushed open the door... to an empty room. The wedding gown swung from its hook on the wall, the layers of lace and satin lifting in the breeze blowing through an open window.

"Oh, God!" Molly was gone, leaving be-

hind her wedding dress with a note pinned
to the bodice. And the name scrawled across
the front of it wasn't the groom's or even
Clayton's. The note his sister had left behind
was addressed to *Abby*. His hand shaking, he
pulled out the pin and shoved the envelope
into the pocket of his jacket.

Every muscle tense, he stalked back into
the sanctuary. Mrs. Hild, at the organ, played
the wedding march. All the guests rose and
turned to face the entrance, where Clayton
stood *alone*. He ignored the murmurs and
the curious stares. He avoided looking at the
groom. He had no idea what to say to Josh
or anyone else but *her*. He focused on Abby.
This was her fault. She'd done exactly what
he'd told her not to do. She'd talked the bride
into running away, just as Abby had run away
eight years ago. She was still a troublemaker.

Chapter Four

The bridal march played on. But no bride walked down the aisle. Only Clayton.

Molly came to her senses. Relief washed over Abby with the realization, easing the knot of apprehension that had tormented her ever since Molly had announced her engagement. During their slumber party at Mrs. Mick's house, she must have gotten through to the nervous bride.

Clayton believed she had, as well. He blamed her. His dark gaze burned into her, and her stomach knotted with new apprehension. And excitement. She had never felt more alive than when she used to get a rise out of Clayton.

No matter what ages they'd been, he'd always seemed so unflappable and in control to Abby. Struggling with her life, Abby had envied that control nearly as much as she'd envied Clayton his family.

At last, Mrs. Hild took notice of the situation and her fingers stilled. The church fell silent, everyone staring at Clayton, while Clayton stared at Abby.

Even though his face was tense, a wry grin touched his mouth. "The wedding is going to be slightly delayed," he said. "The bride is not quite ready yet, so we appreciate your patience. Thank you."

So Molly hadn't left the church—she was just not ready to walk down the aisle? Abby couldn't let Clayton use a sense of obligation or some other excuse to pressure Molly into doing something she really didn't want to do. She bunched her hands in the fabric of her dress, lifting the skirt so she could head down the aisle at a dead run without tripping and falling on her face. She'd already figuratively done that once in front of everyone in Cloverville, when she'd been expelled before graduation.

Clayton, distracted by the way Abby's body moved in the red dress as she ran toward him, nearly let her pass. But then he swallowed hard, suppressing the attraction he felt, and took her arm, linking it through his. He gestured toward Mrs. Hild, who began to play the wedding march again. Abby tugged, but Clayton clasped her closer, forcing her to slow her steps.

"I want to talk to Molly," she said, her voice barely kept to a whisper.

"So do I," he admitted, as they stopped by the door to the empty dressing room.

Abby opened the door, then whirled back toward Clayton, her eyes narrowed accusingly. "Where is she?"

"That's what I'd like to know. Where is she?"

She blinked and then laughed. "She took off?"

"Like you're surprised," he said sardonically, reaching into his pocket for the crumpled note. "You're the only one she left with any explanation."

Abby snatched the envelope from his hand, tore open the flap and pulled out a sheet of paper.

"What does it say?" he asked as she silently read his sister's message. He should have opened the note himself the minute he'd found it. But then his parents had raised him to respect his siblings' privacy. Even so, he curled his hand into a fist so that he wouldn't reach for the paper now and tear it from Abby's hand. "Come on, I'm worried about her. I want to know what it says!"

"It's a good thing that she ran off," Abby said. "Before making the biggest mistake of her life."

Behind them, someone gasped. Clayton turned to face the rest of the wedding party, which had apparently followed them back down the aisle.

"Josh, I'm sorry," he said to Molly's abandoned fiancé.

Color flooded Abby's face and her eyes closed with regret. Then her daughter came closer, chastising her mother. "Mommy, you're not s'posed to run in church. Or talk loud." She cast a disapproving gaze on her mother—and on the ring bearers, too.

"Mommy was bad," Clayton murmured for Abby's ears only. *Very* bad, since he knew she was responsible for Molly's disappearance. Was this her plan all along—to come back to Cloverville and cause as much trouble as she could? Was this her revenge for the way the town—and *Clayton*—had treated her?

Talking Molly out of getting married was far more serious than the tattoos she'd talked her into when they were all a lot younger.

"I'm sorry," Abby said, both to Josh and her daughter. She offered Clayton no apology, however. "She doesn't say that… In the note…about making a mistake. She's just really confused right now."

"What's going on?" Rory asked, tugging loose the knot on his bow tie. "Did Molly really skip out?"

Clayton shrugged his tense shoulders. "Ask Abby. She's the one with the explanation."

Abby's heart filled with mixed emotions. At first she'd simply been relieved that Molly had acknowledged her feelings and changed her mind. Now she contemplated the emotional fallout as she faced the groom and his two young sons.

"Is she all right?" Josh asked, his eyes shining with concern. Any other jilted groom probably would be furious over being left at the altar, but Josh appeared more worried about his runaway bride than his pride.

Abby thought she understood why her friend had accepted his proposal. It was so hard to find a genuinely nice guy. But if Molly didn't absolutely love the man and his sons, she'd done them a favor by leaving before saying "I do."

"She's okay," Abby assured him. "She's just confused right now. She needs some time alone to figure out what she really wants."

"Maybe she should have figured *that* out before she accepted Josh's proposal. It's pretty damned flaky to back out at the altar," the best man grumbled, pushing a hand through his blond hair and then massaging the back of his neck.

"Molly is not flaky." Colleen defended her sister.

Abby saved her breath. She would need it later, to defend herself when Clayton launched his attack. She looked at the open window, tempted to climb over the sill herself. But Lara wouldn't approve of that any more than she had approved of Abby running in church. Sometimes she wondered which of them was the child and which the parent.

The groom probably didn't have that problem with his boys, who were now amusing themselves plucking the petals off each other's boutonnieres. Carnation petals dropped to the carpet like red confetti.

"It's my fault," Josh offered. "I rushed

her into this, even though I knew she wasn't ready."

Nick gripped his friend's shoulder. "Don't blame yourself. She could have told you no. This just goes to show you *they* can't be trusted."

Instead of being offended like Colleen, who gasped at the comment, Abby smiled. Obviously, Nick Jameson had dated women the same caliber as the men she'd dated. She understood his bitterness.

"What are we going to do with all the food?" Mrs. McClintock asked as she joined the rest of the wedding party. "Mrs. George and the Kellys have been cooking for days. We can't let all that food and hard work go to waste."

"Are you serious, Mom?" Colleen asked, apparently stunned by the cool practicality of her mother's question.

Abby wasn't surprised. Mrs. Mick had always been a sensible woman who'd pragmatically handled all the challenges life had thrown at her. She'd survived losing her husband. She'd raised her children to be smart, responsible adults. Like Abby, she actually knew that Molly had a good reason for skipping out before her vows.

Abby wondered which, of the several ones she'd given Molly the night before, was the reason that had compelled her to run. Molly hadn't said in the letter. Although she'd only mentioned two things in her note, she wanted too much. Time alone to sort things out was no problem, but Molly had also asked Abby to stay in Cloverville and wait for her to come back. For how long?

Mrs. McClintock glanced at the slim wristwatch she wore beneath her carnation-and-lily corsage. "The food is already at the reception hall, along with the drinks. It's all already paid for, and we can't cancel."

"We *have* to cancel the reception," Clayton said. "We have to cancel the wedding." *Damn.* As acting father of the bride, that was his responsibility. His earlier stall in the church had been just that—a stall, in the hope that he'd come back to this room and find Molly in her gown and veil, waiting impatiently to walk down the aisle. "I'll go make the announcement to our guests."

"That's not your responsibility," Josh told him.

"You're new." Rory snorted. "You don't know yet that Clayton thinks *everything* and *everyone* is his responsibility."

Clayton clenched his jaw. Rory thought he *chose* to take responsibility for everything? His father's death had left Clayton with no choice.

"We can't let all that food go to waste," Mrs. McClintock insisted.

"Daddy, I'm hungry!" Buzz shouted. His brother's boutonniere had no petals left to distract him.

"When are we having cake?" T.J. asked. "I want cake!" His lower lip began to quiver.

"Aren't we going to have a party?" Lara asked. Her lip didn't quiver, and her eyes remained dry, but the disappointment in her voice touched something deep inside Clayton.

"I did already pay for the food," he acknowledged. He'd insisted on paying Mrs. George and the Kellys up front. Mrs. George supported her family by catering and he hadn't wanted them to put out any of their own money. "Mom's right. We shouldn't let it go to waste. Josh, would it be okay with you if we…"

"If you have my wedding without the bride?" Josh asked. Instead of bitterness, humor laced his voice. Perhaps he hadn't been any readier to get married than Molly. "Only if you let me pay."

"No, that's out of the question," Clayton said. His sister had been the one to back out, and he would be the one to clean up the mess. But he didn't blame Molly. He blamed Abby. Like the groom, however, he wasn't nearly as angry as he should have been. Maybe Abby had done them all a favor. "I'll go and explain the situation to our guests."

"Situation?" Nick repeated. "How are you going to explain this?"

"He's a salesman." Rory once again sang his brother's "praises." "Don't worry, he'll sell it."

And he sold it. Abby couldn't keep the twinkle from her eyes as she remembered his words. "My sister wasn't quite ready for today, but the reception hall *will* be. We'd like for you to join us for dinner, cake, drinks and dancing. And, of course, to laugh over this latest scandal." Nervous chuckles replaced the earlier hushed murmurs. He'd relaxed their guests and tempered the embarrassment.

Now, if only Abby could relax. But pressed tight against Clayton's side, she could barely draw a breath. Lara nudged her, pushing Abby even closer to Clayton as she tried to escape the wrestling ring bearers on the other side of her on the bench seat of the limousine.

Across from Clayton, Rory, Colleen, Nick and Brenna shared the other seat. Alone in the back sat the jilted groom. "So no one's going to uncork the champagne?" Rory asked, gesturing toward a bottle chilling in a bucket of ice.

Colleen jabbed an elbow into her younger brother's ribs. Reacting just as the twins would have, he shoved her over until she nearly wound up on Nick's lap. But the best man moved away in response, inadvertently pushing Brenna onto the floor. The redhead, landing smack on her butt, erupted with laughter.

Abby joined in. Then Colleen started sputtering. Finally Abby felt Clayton's body move as laughter rumbled deep in his chest. Buzz and T.J. dissolved into fits of giggles. Lara, taught not to laugh at others, tried to hold out. But Abby tickled her ribs, and the little girl joined in.

The groom shook his head, then chuckled, too. "What a day…"

"It's not over yet," Brenna warned him as he reached for her hand and helped her onto the seat next to him. "Are you sure you want to do this, the limo, the reception?"

"We're not calling it a reception anymore," Josh reminded her. "It's an open house for the town."

"*We* don't live here," Nick pointed out. "*We* don't need to go."

"Not yet, but we're opening our office in Cloverville," Josh said. "We need to meet our potential patients."

When Abby opened her second office—in Chicago—she'd held just such an open house, inviting all her potential clients. Her first office, in Detroit, had been in a corner of a dumpy motel room. Where should she open her third? During the sleepover, Colleen had tried to convince her that Cloverville needed her business. But Abby didn't need Cloverville. How could she stay here and wait for Molly?

"So can we open the champagne now?" Rory asked his brother.

The grin faded from Clayton's handsome face. "No. And even if we did, you wouldn't get any."

"Come on," Rory argued.

"Rory." Clayton said his brother's name in a way that sounded like a warning—the same way he usually said Abby's name.

Recognizing the tone, she suppressed a smile.

Clayton still thought of her as the screwed-up teenager she hadn't been in such a long time. But then how could he see her as anyone else? He didn't know who she was now, only who she'd been.

What about him? Why did she want to know who *he'd* become? Besides an insurance agent and a big brother, who was he as a man?

"You're lucky you didn't marry into this family," Rory told the groom. "We never have any fun!"

The headache that had started to throb around at Clayton's temples back at the church intensified. He closed his eyes against the pain. But that was a mistake. With his eyes closed, he couldn't see. He could only feel. Abby's body pressed tight against his side. His thigh tensed as her hip rocked against it. The limo turned again and she nearly slid onto his lap. The rest of his body tensed, as well, and he groaned.

"It's not that bad," Abby murmured, her breath warm against his ear as she whispered beneath the other conversations taking place in the limo.

"What?"

"You handled everything really well back at the church," she complimented him.

"You only say that because I didn't wring your neck," he whispered back, unable to fight the grin that was forming. He should be furious with her. Somehow he just knew that if Abby had skipped the wedding as well as the rehearsal, he would have walked Molly down the aisle to her groom and she would have said, "I do." But would she have been happy?

Abby laughed again, softly, her breast jiggling against his arm. He bit back another groan.

"You still blame me," she said, shaking her head. Her hair brushed against his jaw, the scent of lilies enveloping him.

"Tell me you didn't try to talk Molly out of getting married," he challenged her.

"If I did, would you believe me?" she asked.

Who was challenging whom? "Abby..."

Abby's lips curved upward. She leaned closer and murmured, "Don't hurt yourself trying to trust me."

"Abby..."

"I did." The car turned and she shifted even closer.

"What?" With her lips pretty well touching his skin, skimming across his jaw next to his ear, his nerves jumbled, and he'd forgotten what they were talking about.

"I talked Molly into running."

He'd known it the minute he'd found the dressing room empty, even before he'd noticed the note pinned to the dress. But he wasn't nearly as angry with her now as he'd been at that minute.

Oblivious to the other conversations going on around her, Abby focused solely on Clayton and waited for his fury, for some reaction from him. But he leaned back in the seat and lifted his arm to rest along the back. The sleeve of his tuxedo jacket brushed against her bare shoulders.

"You're not mad?" she asked. *She was.* Crazy mad because his proximity had her heart racing, her skin turning rosy pink and her breath growing shallow.

"I'm mad," he stated in a low, flat voice.

"You're not acting mad." Why wasn't he acting mad?

"I can't wring your neck in front of witnesses," he muttered as he closed his eyes, probably imagining her murder. "I'll do that later. When we're alone."

Abby had already vowed to make certain she was never alone with Clayton Mc-Clintock, and not for fear of her neck so much as her heart. She couldn't fall for Clayton. Her love for him now would be just as unrequited as her first crush had been all those years ago.

Guilt nagged at Abby as she stepped into the crowded reception hall. From the ice sculpture to the open bar, Clayton had spared no expense.

"It's so pretty," Lara murmured as she took in the fairy lights and flowers decorating the hall.

"It looks like Christmas," Buzz said, his neck swiveling around as if he were searching for a sleigh and Santa Claus.

Lara shook her head. "Valentine's Day."

With the red-and-white lights and balloons, the decorated hall was at least as romantic as the holiday of love. But Molly hadn't loved the groom or she wouldn't have gone out the window. Abby had to remind herself of that, to keep the guilt from weighing too heavily. *She* hadn't confused Molly; Molly had already been confused and unsure. Until now. And now Molly knew she needed time to sort things out, and she needed Abby to stay here, among so many difficult memories.

The DJ, catching sight of people in red dresses and black tuxes, played a drum roll. "And here's your wedding party!"

Clayton, wildly waving his arms, tried to stop the announcements. But the tables were tucked in tight between the entrance and the dance floor, and he couldn't get around everyone before the DJ began to call out their names. Brenna hadn't bothered to line them up as she had at the church, so no one was called by the appropriate name as the introductions were read. He'd gotten to the bride and groom by the time Clayton finally reached him, slamming a hand over the mike too late.

The speakers screeched. As Clayton whispered to the DJ, the guy's face flushed bright red. Then Clayton took his hand from the mike and spoke into it. "Thank you all for joining us. Cloverville has been long overdue for a party. We really don't need an occasion to get together with our friends and neighbors and have a community celebration."

"Weddings and funerals," Rory grumbled from near Abby. "That's what this town thinks is a party."

The teenager should have been able to remember his father's funeral, unless the memories had been so painful he'd suppressed them. No one had been celebrating then. Abby couldn't remember a dry eye in the church. Except for Clayton. He'd just been a boy, really, but he'd tried so hard to act the man in his father's place, being a strong and steady pillar for his grieving family. Even when she'd resented his assumption of authority over her and her friends, Abby had always admired him for that.

"We actually do have an occasion," Mrs. McClintock said, joining her son on the dance floor. "Let's make this a Welcome Home, Abby and Lara Hamilton party."

Abby's heart warmed. Mrs. Mick was such a sweetheart. But Clayton obviously didn't think so. Even from a distance, Abby noted the muscle that jumped in his cheek as he clenched his jaw. He'd been willing to pay for a community open house, maybe because he could use it as a tax write-off. But he wasn't happy about bankrolling a welcome home party for her.

Lara tugged on Abby's hand. Her voice quavering with excitement, she asked, "Mommy, the party's for us?"

"Oh, honey..." She rarely had to tell her daughter no, because Lara never wanted much.

But Clayton spared her the trouble when

he said, "Yes, the party's for Abby and Lara Hamilton." He stopped, cleared his throat and said, "Welcome home to Cloverville."

What did Mrs. Mick have on her oldest that she'd managed with just a raised brow to get him to change his mind? Abby had to find out.

The guests all turned toward her and ap-plauded, pulling Abby's gaze away from Clayton. She glanced around at the people who had just about run her out of Clover-ville eight years earlier. The way they sur-rounded her brought to mind old nightmares about a lynching. She had no doubt they'd almost considered it over the damage to the colonel. They'd been furious then. What had changed to make them clap for her today?

Resentment and bitterness over the past rose, threatening to choke her. But Lara squeezed her hand. Her blue eyes shimmered with excitement. Abby struggled to suppress her negative feelings. She couldn't call these people hypocrites, not in front of her daughter. She couldn't ruin Lara's joy at their "party." So she forced a smile.

Clayton's jaw unclenched, his tension eas-ing as he took note of Abby's stress. She hadn't wanted to come back to Cloverville at all, let alone be the center of attention again. He'd wrung her neck without lifting a finger. The townspeople descended on her now, more than they had at the church. Probably asking questions about her life after Cloverville.

He wanted to get close enough to overhear. He wanted to know what she'd been up to the past eight years besides having and raising Lara. But he wanted to know about Lara, too. And he had no doubt that the town busybodies were nosy enough to ask questions that were far too personal. They certainly never hesitated to ask him why *he* hadn't settled down yet. Some of the gossips were worse than his matchmaking mother.

His mom pressed a kiss to his cheek. "You did a good thing."

"*You* did," he reminded her as he escorted her off the dance floor. "Changing the party to their honor was *your* idea."

"But you're paying for it," she said with a chuckle.

He sighed, disgusted with himself for not taking up the groom on the many offers he'd made to pay for the wedding and reception. Even as they'd climbed out of the limo, Josh had offered, no, insisted, on paying for everything—*after* Molly had left him at the altar.

Clayton shook his head. She'd better have a damn good reason for jilting such a nice guy.

He had to talk to his sister and find out what had changed her mind. He already knew *who* had facilitated the decision. His gaze found Abby in the middle of the guests, her eyes wide with surprise—probably over his agreement to change the reception into a party for her and Lara. From the minute he'd picked her up at the airport, he hadn't exactly acted as if he was happy to see her again.

But he found it easier to agree with his mother than argue with her. He didn't want to upset her anymore.

She patted his arm. "Honey, Mrs. George—the caterer—is trying to get your attention."

But someone else had his attention instead. He pulled his gaze from Abby and focused on his mom. With a smile brightening her brown eyes and illuminating her face, she didn't seem all that upset about the cancelled wedding. "Mom…"

She kissed his cheek again. "Your father would be so proud of how you've handled everything."

And that was why he'd insisted on paying for the wedding, because that was what his father would have wanted. It was what Dad would have done if he were alive. Clayton reached for his checkbook. "I'll take care of Mrs. George." The woman had worked hard to make the old American Legion hall look festive, and he wanted to compensate her efforts. But before he walked away, he kissed his mother's cheek. "You look beautiful today."

That was the other thing his father would have done, the thing he'd never failed to do every day. Tell his wife how beautiful she was.

Clayton's heart clenched as he remembered the depth of his parents' love. Maybe that was why Molly wanted time alone to figure out what she really wanted—she'd realized she didn't love Josh the way their mom had loved their dad. Or maybe she had remembered her mother's inconsolable grief when he'd died and she'd realized nothing was worth the risk of that much pain.

A short while later, his fingers and his bank account in pain from paying off the DJ, the bartender and the photographer, he tucked his checkbook back into the inside pocket of his jacket. He scanned the reception hall for Abby, and came upon her daughter instead, near the cake. Tears welling in her huge blue eyes, Lara stared up at the top of the flower-studded tiers.

"Hey, honey, what's wrong?" he asked, crouching down.

She pointed toward the top of the cake, where the plastic groom stood alone in his black tux. "She's…" Her breath hitched. "Gone."

The little plastic bride, as well as the real one. How appropriate.

"I don't know where she is, honey."

The plastic one *or* the real one, although he suspected Abby knew where his sister was. He had to get a look at the note Molly had left her, because he knew better than to trust that Abby Hamilton had shared everything her friend had written.

"The boys say they have the bride," she said, her voice trembling, "and they're going to flush her."

"Flush her?"

"Down…down the toilet." Her breath hitched again. One tear spilled from her eye and trailed down her cheek.

"Where are they?" Clayton wasn't all that upset that these two young hellions were not going to be his stepnephews. But without pressure from Abby, Molly might realize what she wanted was to marry Josh. And he'd have to learn how to deal with the rambunctious duo.

"The boys are in…in…the bathroom."

Clayton brushed her tear away with his thumb. "It's okay, honey."

"They said she was me, that they're flushing *me* down the toilet."

He couldn't remember what the little plastic bride had looked like. He hadn't paid any attention to the cake or anything else to do with the wedding—he'd only paid for it.

Ah, hell, he didn't care about the money. He could make more. He *knew* how to do that, but what he didn't know how to do was make Lara feel better.

Another tear spilled from an eye, clinging to her dense black lashes before dropping onto his thumb. The vise tightened around his heart even more. He looked away from her, turning his attention to the cake. The five-tiered cake—frosted white and adorned with red and white sugar flowers—rose high above them.

"Honey, there's no way the boys got the bride down." They would have tipped over the table and knocked the cake to the floor. And not a single frosting flower had been disturbed. Then he peered closer and noticed that a few were missing from the bottom tier, miniature fingerprints left behind in the frosting.

She blinked those thick lashes, dispersing her tears. "You don't think so?"

"See how big the cake is?"

She nodded, the carnations and lilies rustling in her hair as her curls bounced. "It's so pretty."

Like Lara. And her mother.

"If they had tried to get her down, they would have knocked the whole cake over, honey. There's no way they have her. They're just teasing you."

Because boys tease girls they like.

Was that why he'd been giving Abby such a hard time, why he'd always given her such a hard time? He'd like to think he was more mature than that now and that he had been even all those years ago. He'd like to think he was too smart to be attracted to her, too. But he couldn't keep lying to himself. Even now he knew if he lifted his gaze from her daughter, he'd start searching the crowded hall for Abby.

"They were *teasing* me?" Her voice trembled, but with anger this time, making her sound much older than her tender years. Making her sound like her mother.

"Afraid so."

Lara tilted her chin and narrowed her eyes,

anger stiffening her small, thin body. The boys were going to pay for picking on Lara Hamilton.

He almost felt sorry for the twins. If they were smart, they'd go on hiding out in the men's room. As he glanced around the reception hall, he didn't see them among the guests, but he did notice the party favors, packages of chocolate-coated cookies, missing from the tables nearby. Either they were stealing the treats from the other tables by now, or they'd eaten so many cookies they'd gotten sick.

Lara turned those expressive eyes on him, pinning him with her determined gaze. "Mr. Mick, can I ask you something?"

Mr. Mick? Damn Abby.

"Sure, Lara." But he had no idea where the plastic bride was.

"Are you my daddy?"

Chapter Five

Lara's question stole his breath away, leaving him gasping. He hadn't even kissed Abby yet. *Yet?* He'd thought about it ever since she'd returned to Cloverville. Hell, he'd thought about kissing her eight years ago, when she'd been a rebellious teen and he'd been a too-old-for-her-and-for-his-years college student. But he'd resisted then because she'd been more trouble than he could have handled.

And now that she was a mother, he certainly had no intention of getting involved with her. He'd already, at least partly, raised three younger siblings. He couldn't take on someone else's responsibility, too. Between the insurance agency and his family, as his girlfriend Ellen had pointed out, he had nothing left to give. Lara deserved more, even if he wasn't sure yet what Abby deserved.

"Mr. Mick?" she asked, blinking watery eyes at him.

His stomach flipped. She was such a sweet little girl. "Call me Clayton, honey," he told her. Not Daddy. He had no intention of *ever* being called Daddy.

"So you're not…" She trailed off, nibbling on her bottom lip.

His heart twisted. "Why would you ask me that, honey?"

What had Abby told her daughter?

Color flushed Lara's face, painting her cheeks bright pink. "Mommy told me that my daddy was someone she knew a long time ago."

And at the airport she'd introduced Clayton as someone she'd known a long time ago.

"How old are you?" he asked Lara.

"I'll be five, October second."

Four years old and she was this smart? Abby had never done all that well in school. If she hadn't been expelled, she probably still wouldn't have graduated. How had she had a child so smart, so mature? *Who* was the little girl's father? And where the hell was he, that Lara hadn't ever met the man?

"I haven't seen your mother in eight years, honey." His voice rasped with emotion as he told her, "I'm not your daddy."

"But…" As Lara's gaze rose above where he crouched in front of her, her eyes widened.

Clayton turned his head, peering over his shoulder into Abby's face, as pale with shock as if she'd seen a ghost. Of course with her return to Cloverville, she'd probably already had to face down a phantom or two from her past. Hell, he'd been the one to show her the colonel. A laugh bubbled up in his throat, but he controlled it, not wanting to hurt Lara's feelings. Hoping he hadn't already.

Abby cleared her throat. "Lara, sweetheart, we have to eat dinner before we can have any cake."

Memories of dinners she'd eaten with his family years ago flashed through Clayton's mind. To Abby, dessert had always been the main course. He let out a derisive snort, but Abby didn't even look at him. Her focus remained on her daughter. Maybe she had changed.

"I know, Mommy," Lara said, her voice soft.

"The food is being served at our table now."

She extended her hand, reaching for her daughter as if to snatch her away from Clayton.

He should have been glad that she was rescuing him from an awkward situation. Instead, he felt as if she were *rescuing* her daughter from him, as if she didn't trust him. He hadn't been very nice to Abby when they were kids. He'd been so angry over his father's illness and his own inability to help that he'd lashed out at the one person who wasn't hurting in the way the rest of his family had been hurting. But now, looking back, he realized Abby had been hurting, too. She'd loved his father. Probably more than she'd loved her own father.

Abby didn't want Lara away from Clayton. *She* wanted to get away from him. A charming Clayton was far more dangerous than the usual uptight, judgmental one. Good thing she'd made certain she and Lara were seated at the other end of the wedding party table from the only open chair left, which was for Clayton.

But Lara, who'd always been so obedient, didn't put her hand in Abby's. Instead, she put it on Clayton's shoulder. "Will you look for her?" she asked.

He nodded solemnly. "Of course."

Why was he being so nice to her daughter? Abby doubted it was the reason some other men had been nice to Lara—in order to get close to her mother. She knew Clayton didn't want to be any closer to her than she did to him. He didn't even want her in the same town.

Oh, Molly.

Abby couldn't leave until she talked to Molly and knew she was really all right. Like Colleen and Brenna, she'd been using her cell phone to call their runaway friend, but Molly had been serious about needing time alone to think. Her cell was turned off, leaving Abby to field the nosy questions of all those people who, like Clayton, had once wanted her gone. Although she'd been trapped in a series of intrusive conversations, she'd never shifted her attention from her daughter, too used to living in a big city where she could never let down her guard. Could she do that here?

Not with Clayton around.

"Who do you have Clayton looking for?" she asked Lara as she led her away from the man who still crouched in front of the cake table. Although she'd once loved sweets, the man before the table inspired more hunger in her right now than the lavish cake. *No.* She couldn't give in to her attraction to Clayton McClintock. It was bad enough that she'd admitted it.

"Clayton's going to find the bride," her daughter answered.

No wonder he'd agreed so readily to help. He wanted to talk to Molly, too. But did he want to make sure his sister was all right or did he want to force her to go through with a loveless marriage?

Abby would have believed every marriage in the world was loveless, if not for having witnessed Clayton's parents' love for each other. Their relationship had been special and rare. But Abby was too realistic to hope for that for herself, knowing she'd only find more disappointment.

What about Clayton? Did he believe in love?

Clayton reached for the plastic cup. He really needed a drink, despite the champagne toast he'd just had. Or maybe because of it. He'd toasted Abby Hamilton's return to Cloverville. She wasn't even off the plane before she'd started messing up his life, getting him dumped, arguing with him and undermining the wedding. She was still nothing but trouble. But he honestly couldn't blame her for everything that had gone wrong, even though he wanted to. He wanted any reason to squelch the desire he felt for her.

Hell, he didn't actually miss Erin… Ellen. *He* couldn't even remember the woman's name now, not since Abby had come home. But she wasn't staying. She'd sworn she was leaving after the wedding. So would she be gone tomorrow? For some reason the thought brought him no relief, only that familiar tight feeling in his chest.

"Hey!" Rory shouted in protest as his brother pulled the cup from his hand.

Clayton sniffed the rim.

"It…it's just punch," Rory insisted.

Clayton tipped the cup and swallowed a mouthful, wincing and grimacing as the fiery liquid burned a trail down his throat. He blinked twice to clear his eyes before remarking, "Since when is nonalcoholic punch hundred proof? Oh, yeah, since I noticed your friends, the Hendrix boys, hanging out by the punch bowl."

"It's spiked?" Rory asked, his eyes widening in feigned shock. "Mrs. George or the bartender must have done it by accident."

Clayton shook his head, glad he'd kept an eye on the Hendrix brothers, which hadn't been easy since Abby, in that strapless red dress, kept drawing his attention away. Before following Rory out the side door with his cup, he'd told the bartender to pull the bowl. With luck, no one else had taken a glass of the spiked punch yet. The Hendrix boys, catching sight of Clayton heading toward them, had taken off, leaving Rory to fend for himself. "Those kids are bad news, Rory."

"They're my friends."

The same argument, eight years before, flashed through his mind. Molly and Colleen defending their friendship with Abby Hamilton, when he'd dragged them all out of a tattoo parlor in Grand Rapids.

"You're only fourteen. You shouldn't be hanging out with kids that old." Or that much trouble.

"I'm almost fifteen—same age as Chad."

"But Greg is seventeen." Old enough to drive too fast and recklessly. Clayton had already forbidden Rory to ride with him. But then he'd also forbidden him to drink or smoke. He tossed the cup into a Dumpster in the alley. Then he put a hand on Rory, reaching inside his brother's tux for the pack of cigarettes he found in the pocket. How the hell were these kids getting their hands on cigarettes and booze?

"I was just holding those for Greg."

Clayton shook his head again. "Rory, I'm not buying it and neither will Sheriff Block."

The boy's eyes goggled in real surprise. "You'd turn me in?"

"You're too old to turn over my knee."

"You're not my father!"

No. He wasn't. And that was the problem. Despite knowing his father the shortest amount of time, Rory still missed his dad, and he resented his older siblings for having had more time with him. Clayton understood, and he felt for the kid. That was probably why he, like their mother, had been too easy on him. Rory was the single biggest reason why he didn't want to take on any other responsibility. He was failing the kid and failing his dad, who'd asked him to look after the family.

Someone cleared his throat before joining them outside. Clayton turned his attention to Mr. Schipper, his old teacher and Rory's current English teacher. "Hey, guys, your mother's looking for you both."

Usually Mr. Schipper, with his graying hair and mustache, was looking for Mrs. McClintock, as well. Clayton had noticed the older man's interest in his mother. While he knew his mom deserved some happiness after losing her husband, he hadn't stopped to analyze how *he* really felt about his mom getting involved with another man.

Rory pulled away and ran back inside the hall. He had obviously made his decision.

The teacher sighed. "I haven't had a student give me as hard a time as Rory since…"

"Abby Hamilton?"

"I was going to say Greg Hendrix. Abby was a challenge, too," the teacher admitted, "but she really wasn't a bad kid."

And Rory was. Ellen had been smart to dump him—Clayton would never have time for a personal life. That was good though, since he had no room for serious involvements in his plan.

"I'm sorry I couldn't find the bride," Clayton said as he held Lara in his arms. Her feet dangled above his as he whirled her around the dance floor.

She giggled. "It's okay."

After busting his brother, he'd looked. Clayton had really wanted to find that figurine for her, probably selfishly so that he would feel as if he'd succeeded at *something*. Most especially he'd wanted to make Lara smile. But she didn't really want that plastic doll. She wanted a daddy. He couldn't help her with that; not without letting her down more than he had anyone else.

He should find his brother again and make sure he hadn't snuck any more alcohol. But with the Hendrix boys gone, maybe Clayton could relax. Those kids were nothing but trouble. Like someone else he knew.

Deep red nails lightly tapped his shoulder. "I'd like to cut in."

She obviously didn't see him as a father figure for her child, either. She had already danced with her daughter, spinning her around and around while they both smiled and laughed.

As he turned to leave the dance floor, she caught his arm. "Wait a minute."

Unconcerned about her red satin dress, she knelt in front of Lara and kissed her cheek. "Mrs. Mick is going to take you home, sweetheart. It's getting late. I'll be back before you go to bed, though, to tuck you in."

"Can Clayton tuck me in?" she asked.

"He doesn't live at Mrs. Mick's."

But even if he did, Clayton doubted Abby would let him tuck her daughter into bed. She probably thought he'd be as mean to Lara as he'd been to her.

He crouched down to meet the child's gaze,

her eyes soft and sleepy. "Good night, Lara. You were a beautiful flower girl."

"Miniature bride," Abby corrected him, while her daughter threw her arms around Clayton's neck and hugged him tight.

Shocked by the girl's affection, Clayton patted Lara's back, his hand feeling too big and clumsy to handle someone so small and delicate. Just like his mother, and like so many guests tonight, she pressed a kiss to his cheek. His heart tightened.

"Thank you, Clayton," she said.

For the dance? For looking for the bride? She didn't clarify before walking off the dance floor to join his mother. That vise tightened around Clayton's emotions even more as Lara waved at him before putting her hand in his mother's. His mom's eyes softened as she beamed down at her.

"Uh-oh," he murmured as he rose from his crouch. His mother was in love. No doubt she would renew her pressure on her eldest to give her a grandchild or, more specifically, to give her *that* grandchild. His mother wouldn't have cared if Molly had gone through the wedding and provided her with a slew of grandkids. Mary McClintock had another plan, and a not very subtle one, to fix him up with Abby Hamilton.

Warm fingers wrapped around his hand as Abby stepped into his arms. His body jerked and surprise shot through him. "What the—"

"I cut in on my daughter, Clayton, so I could dance with you," Abby told him, smiling at his stunned reaction to Lara's show of affection and then hers. Not that she was really showing him affection. She'd only wanted to talk to him to thank him for how sweet he'd been to Lara.

Clayton stared down at her, his eyes darkening. Then his fingers closed over hers, his other hand slid to the small of her back and her smile slipped away. She stiffened now, so that she wouldn't melt into the enticing hardness of his body.

What had made her think dancing with Clayton McClintock would be a good idea? The song ended, and she relaxed slightly. But Clayton didn't release her. He just held her, in the middle of the dance floor. Before she could pull away, the next song started, slower and smokier than the previous one.

Clayton's hand on her back pushed her closer, so that her breasts settled against his chest, her thighs and hips pressed tight to his. She swallowed hard.

"What a day...." Clayton murmured into her hair, his breath warm against her ear.

Her nerve endings tingled as she followed his lead. Weariness settled over her after all she'd just done: packing up her apartment in Chicago, catching the flight and getting through an emotional confrontation with Molly. With a sigh of defeat, she leaned her head on Clayton's shoulder and dragged in a breath of air scented with citrus and musk, a mixture of aftershave and Clayton. "I hope Molly's all right."

"Me, too."

"You don't want to wring her neck?" she asked, surprised by his admission. But he'd already surprised her in that he hadn't searched her purse for Molly's note. Apparently he intended to honor his sister's request for time alone.

"I don't want to wring her neck."

"Just mine?" she asked.

"Not anymore."

"You got your revenge by making me the guest of honor," she surmised, turning her head to witness the grin spreading across his face, etching creases in his cheeks. When he grinned like that, her knees trembled.

"Abby Hamilton, the guest of honor."

"More like the guest of dishonor," she grumbled, shaking off the bitterness.

Somehow, the townspeople seemed more willing to let go of the past than she did. She needed to believe they still hated her. If they didn't, she had no excuse for staying away. And now, eight years later, she wondered if they had really hated her as much as she'd imagined. Or was she the one who had hated her life? Hated herself?

"I didn't ask you to dance in order to fight with you," she said. "I wanted to thank you for being so kind to Lara."

"She's a sweet kid."

Pride swelled in her chest. "Yes, she is."

"Nothing like you were."

No, Abby had been more like the groom's twin sons. A hyper little brat. "I've been blessed."

"She asked me a question," Clayton said.

Abby's heart slammed against her ribs. She'd overheard her daughter's question and been too shocked to intervene before Clayton had answered her. "I know." She'd been completely mortified. "Thank you for handling that so well."

"She took me by surprise. She has no idea who her father is?" From the way he gazed down at her, he obviously wondered if Abby knew.

"I've never been in love," she said, reminding him of their conversation the night before. "But I don't indiscriminately sleep around."

"Just discriminately?"

She tried to pull away, but his hand at her back held her tight against him.

"I'm just teasing you, Abby," he said, his hand stroking her spine as one might smooth the raised hair of a spooked cat. "Relax."

She doubted that was something she'd ever be able to do in his arms, with the heat of his body burning through his clothes and hers, setting her senses afire. She tingled everywhere.

"Now who's the uptight one?" he teased.

He hadn't been the first to call her uptight. She'd never slept around. "I don't like talking about my personal life."

But that hadn't stopped everyone in town from asking her personal questions. She'd been able to handle their nosiness, though, only giving them the information she wanted to share. About her business. The employment agency for specialized temps. Nothing personal. The problem with Clayton was that Abby wanted to share more with him. She wanted to prove to him she wasn't the out-of-control girl she'd once been.

"There are no secrets in a small town," Clayton reminded her.

"I know." That was why she hadn't wanted to come back.

But at least now, from listening to all the gossip, she knew about Clayton, about how hard he'd worked not only to keep his father's business but also to expand it. She also knew about the other duties of his father's that he'd assumed—city councilman, Rotary Club president and school board member. No wonder he hadn't found time to fall in love.

"I don't intend to stay," she stated.

"You're going home in the morning?" he asked, his tone guarded.

She'd expected him to be more hopeful or relieved that she was leaving. She hated to burst his bubble of anticipation. "I'm going to stay a little longer than I planned."

"You're going to wait until you hear from Molly, to make sure she's okay?"

She nodded, moving her head against his

shoulder, and waited for him to ask about the note. She had no doubt that he wanted to read it, that he wouldn't trust her to relay Molly's entire message.

But the question he asked surprised her. "So are you ever going to answer Lara's question?"

"About her father?" She tensed. "I don't know. How do you tell a child that her father didn't want her?" Her parents had usually told her that when they were drunk, hurling the accusation at her just like the empty beer cans and cigarette butts they'd tossed around. She hadn't asked to be born, and she hadn't planned to ruin their lives. But still they'd blamed her, just like everyone else. And she never wanted Lara to feel the way she had.

His hand slid from her back as he wrapped his arm tightly around her, as if he were hugging her. But Clayton McClintock wasn't a hugger. "He actually said that?"

"He gave me money." Emotion choked her throat. She couldn't say what he'd given her the money for. She couldn't think about what he'd wanted her to do.

"Oh, Abby." He leaned his forehead against hers. His face so close, they only had to move a hairsbreadth for their lips to touch, to taste.

Abby drew in a shuddery breath. "It's okay. His loss."

"A big loss." Of both Lara and Abby. Clayton pulled back at the thought, surprised he'd come so close to kissing Abby Hamilton. Again. He'd almost kissed her the night before, as well. He'd leaned so close then that he'd tasted her breath against his lips.

"What kind of man shirks his responsibilities?" He couldn't fathom walking away, despite all the times he'd been tempted to run.

"You'd be surprised," she murmured.

"Oh, I can imagine your type." Exciting. She'd never go for someone boring. Abby would need someone who could hold her attention, who could challenge and stimulate her. "Some bad-boy type. A biker. Or a lead singer in a rock band."

A laugh sputtered out of her. Her smile stole his breath away. "Actually, Lara's father was a lot like you."

"What?"

"A man I thought I could trust." Or she never would have slept with him. "He was an insurance adjuster."

"I'm an insurance *agent*," he said. "Big difference." But his lips lifted in a grin as he mocked himself. "I really figured you for a biker babe."

"Leather miniskirt? Tattoos?" Would his opinion of her ever change? He was determined to think the worst of her.

His throat moved as he swallowed hard, then nodded.

She'd almost gotten a tattoo. Back in high school she'd talked Molly, Brenna, Colleen and their friend Eric into going to a tattoo parlor in Grand Rapids. But Clayton, home from college for the weekend and working on a tip from Rory, had tracked them down before Abby had been able to get hers. Of course, when she'd seen the needles, she'd been magnanimous and had insisted everyone else go before her.

"It's your fault I don't have a tattoo," she reminded him. He'd told the tattoo artist that she wasn't eighteen yet, and she hadn't been able to prove him wrong.

He grinned slightly. "You could have gone back after your birthday."

"Other things were going on then." Her expulsion. Clayton's dad dying.

"So, no tattoos?"

She shook her head.

"No leather?"

She bit her lip. "I didn't say that."

His grin grew, creasing his cheeks again as his eyes lit up. She never would have guessed that when she came back for Molly's wedding she would wind up flirting with Clayton McClintock.

"I have a leather jacket," she teased him, and then she sighed as if bored with herself. "So, no tattoos. No leather miniskirts. You don't know me at all, Clayton."

She was right—he didn't know her. But he suddenly realized that he wanted to. Who had Abby Hamilton become once she left Cloverville, besides a mother? Who was she as a *woman?*

"And I'm not going to be around long enough for you to get to know me. *Your* loss."

Last night she'd sworn she was leaving right after the wedding. Even if she hung around town a couple more days waiting to hear from Molly, she wasn't staying longer. There was no risk of involvement.

With his knuckles under her chin, he tilted up her face. Her lips lifted in that sassy smile she'd always flashed at him. Eight years ago he'd been tempted to wipe that smirk away. For the first time in a long time, Clayton gave in to temptation.

He dipped his head and brushed his lips across hers. She tasted sweet, like the buttercream frosting on the five-tier wedding cake. Clayton had never had much of an appetite for sweets until now. But suddenly he couldn't get enough. He deepened the kiss, sliding his tongue between her soft, silky lips.

Abby melted against him, her body trembling in his arms. When he lifted his head, she blinked up at him, dazed.

"Clayton…"

"It's been a long day." And now he'd lost his mind along with his control. He had no business kissing Abby Hamilton in the middle of a dance floor, surrounded by the entire town of Cloverville. His clients, his neighbors, his friends, his family.

He swallowed a groan. He would never live *this* down. He could almost understand how she felt about the statue of Colonel Clover still standing as evidence of her youthful indiscretion. But while she would leave again, Clayton was like the colonel, a permanent fixture in Cloverville. He only hoped that she'd leave town before she ran him down and broke him like she had the colonel.

Chapter Six

Just as she had in the church, Abby gathered up her skirt and ran.

Well, she couldn't quite manage a run, not as she bumped into dancing couples and spinning children, like a pinball bouncing off the flippers in the machine in the back of the Cloverville pool hall. She smiled and murmured, "Excuse me," and hoped that no one would notice she was fleeing the man who was standing alone in the middle of the dance floor.

Still tempted to race back to him, to kiss him again, she turned away and pushed through the guests. When people tried to stop her, she just smiled and shook her head. She wouldn't be stopped by the busybodies who either wanted to interrogate her or sing Clayton's praises.

Her lips still tingling from his kiss, she could sing praises of her own. Who would have known Clayton McClintock kissed like that? She'd imagined many times, in her misspent youth, what it might feel like to have his mouth pressed to hers. But even her vivid imagination hadn't come close to the reality.

She grabbed her purse from the wedding party table and dashed toward the exit, grateful that the reception hall was close enough so that she could walk back to Mrs. Mick's house. She needed air; she needed to clear her head.

"What are you doing?" someone asked in a low but thoroughly feminine voice.

Brenna. Of course she'd catch Abby. She'd always been the mother among their group of friends, taking care of everyone else. They'd all figured she would be the first to marry and have children—many, many children. But at twenty-six she was still single, her only offspring the various branches of her parents' bakery she'd opened since taking over the business.

The door Abby had just pushed open provided a glimpse of the tree-lined street, the setting sun shining through branches. Then it swung shut, leaving Abby inside and faced with the consequences of kissing Clayton Mc-Clintock. Brenna had to think she'd lost her mind. Abby drew in a shaky breath before turning to face her friend. "What do you mean?"

"Are you leaving already?"

Her breath escaped in a ragged sigh. Apparently Brenna hadn't witnessed the kiss, nor had she heard about it yet.

"I promised Lara I'd tuck her in." Even though her daughter would prefer to have Clayton say good-night.

Longing dimmed Brenna's bright green eyes. It was so obvious she wanted a child of her own. "Of course. She's sleeping in a strange bed. You need to be with her."

Abby's heart softened with concern for her friend. As much as Brenna loved kids, she should have several by now. But the voluptuous redhead had had even more trouble dating than Abby had. After discussing their misadventures, they'd both decided dating wasn't worth the effort better spent on other areas of their lives. Perhaps that was why they'd both been so successful in their work.

Abby pulled Brenna close for a commiserating hug. "You'll find someone," she murmured into her friend's ear.

The woman pulled back, her eyes wide with shock.

"What?" Abby questioned Brenna's wide-eyed stare.

"Abby Hamilton sounding like a romantic?"

"Blame it on the wedding," she said. As her gaze returned to the man standing on the edge of the dance floor, she knew whom to blame for her odd mood.

"The wedding that wasn't," Colleen said as she joined them. "That's what everyone's calling it."

Someone opened the door behind Abby, and cool air rushed over her skin, raising goose bumps. She'd come so close to escaping. But Colleen must have witnessed or heard about Abby's weak moment.

If she had, the girl kept her secret; and it wasn't the only secret she and Abby shared. "So you think Molly's really okay?" Colleen asked. "That she just needs time, like her note said?"

Abby's guilt increased. Instead of thinking about Molly, she'd been thinking about her friend's brother. She reached into her purse and checked her cell phone. "No messages."

Brenna shook her head. "I think she meant that she needed more than a few hours."

Colleen sighed. "She also said she wanted time *alone*. Do you really believe she's alone? When I called Eric, he said he hadn't seen her, but…"

"Eric would lie for her," Brenna said of their fourth friend, the one who'd skipped the wedding entirely. They'd all called him, but he claimed he hadn't seen the runaway bride.

"He'd do more than lie," Abby reminded them. She doubted that much had changed in eight years.

"So we're pretty sure we know where she is," Brenna agreed. "What do we do now?"

"Nothing." Which was exactly what Abby intended to do about Clayton. She'd be gone soon, and they'd never have to see each other again. Unlike the rest of his family, he had never come to visit her since she'd left town. He'd never even called. Despite the kiss, she doubted anything had really changed between them.

"What?" Brenna's voice went deep when she asked the question, as if she were in pain.

"I told you what her note said," Abby said. She hadn't shown it to them—they didn't need to know that Molly wanted her to stay.

She wasn't sure she could fulfill that particular request, but she fully intended to honor Molly's first request and make sure that everyone else honored Molly's request for time alone, too. "Ever since her dad died, she's been so focused on college and then on medical school. She's pushed herself so hard that I think maybe she just burned out. She wants time alone to think, and with luck she'll rest and figure out what she really wants."

"But she's probably not alone," Colleen reminded them. She'd always been a little jealous of Eric's interest in her older sister. Heck, she'd always been a little jealous of Molly, who'd always been so close to perfect.

Abby had thought being bad was tough, but it had probably been worse to be Molly and have that constant pressure to be the best. She wasn't surprised that Mol had finally cracked and run away. Abby had had a lot less pressure and had run a lot longer ago.

"If she's not alone—" a smile tugged at Abby's lips "—there's even less reason to worry about her. She's safe. She's fine. She'll be back when she's ready."

Brenna sighed. "I hope she doesn't take as long as you did to come home."

Abby would have protested that she *wasn't*

home, but she could see Clayton moving through the crowd toward them. "I have to go," she told her friends, before vanishing through the open door.

A headache pounded behind Clayton's eyes, nagging like a hangover despite the fact he'd had only one glass of champagne the night before, when he'd toasted Abby's return. Then, of course, he'd also had that sip of Rory's punch. But the hangover wasn't from drinking. He was hungover from the kiss.

He hadn't slept at all. He'd have liked to blame Molly, because he'd been too worried about her to sleep. Or Rory, for continually testing him. Or maybe he just wasn't used to having a houseguest. The best man, Nick Jameson, had slept in Clayton's spare room, since it had been too late for him to drive back to Grand Rapids after the reception.

With a cup of fresh-brewed coffee in his hand, Clayton headed to the loft's living room with the two-story-high windows looking down on Main Street. The first rays of morning sun reflected off the glass, momentarily blinding Clayton. Not that there was anything to see this early on a Sunday morning. No one was even up for church yet.

Squinting, Clayton peered out through the slats of his wooden blinds. While nothing moved on the street below his apartment, he caught sight of movement farther down, in Mrs. Hild's yard. The old woman knelt on her grass, trimming the bushes around the Cloverville city limits sign.

That wasn't unusual, since Mrs. Hild always rose early to tend her flowers. Seeing her wasn't what jolted Clayton so much that coffee sloshed over the rim of his cup and scalded his hand.

Someone was helping the older woman, bending over to pull weeds from the dirt. That someone wore short shorts that exposed toned legs—surprisingly long legs for such a petite woman. When she straightened up, a curly blond ponytail swung down across the back of her white tank top.

"Damn you, Abby." He shifted the cup to shake the coffee off his burning hand. What the hell was she doing up so early? Hadn't she been able to sleep, either? Had their kiss kept her awake, too?

God, he hoped so.

A shrill whistle drew his attention from Abby to the man who stood next to him, peering through the wooden slats, as well. "Is

that the blonde you were kissing last night?"
Nick Jameson asked. Having slept in his tuxedo pants and pleated dress shirt, the doctor
looked pretty rumpled.

Clayton wasn't the only one who'd had a
rough night. "You saw that?"

"Only because I was dancing near you."

"You were dancing?" Clayton hadn't realized the best man had brought a date to the
wedding.

"With your sister."

For a second Clayton's heart eased with
relief, then he realized Nick was referring to
Colleen and not Molly. Molly was still gone.
"Damn."

"Yeah, damn," the doctor agreed as he stared
through the blinds at Abby in her shorts. "So
she's your girlfriend?"

Clayton tilted the slats. "No, she's an old
friend of my sisters'."

Nick nodded. "Right, that's why Molly left
the note for her. What did it say in it?"

He wasn't about to admit he hadn't seen it.
He'd berated himself already, and he didn't
need to listen to anyone else's recriminations.
Besides which, he believed Abby had shared
everything that was important. "She read what

it said, that Molly wanted some time alone to sort things out."

"So you and the blonde, that kiss on the dance floor... You were trying to get it out of her where the bride ran off to?"

"What?"

"You were turning on the charm."

He hadn't tried charm. Threats, yes—at the church he'd threatened to wring her neck. But the kiss? He wasn't sure what the kiss had been besides a moment of insanity. "That wouldn't work with Abby."

"I don't know. She seemed into you."

Abby Hamilton into *him?* "Yeah, right."

"Too bad."

Regret tightened Clayton's chest. He shouldn't be disappointed. He didn't want Abby Hamilton "into" him. He didn't want to be into Abby Hamilton, either. But he itched to open up the blinds again and watch her as she helped the older woman in her garden.

"Not too bad at all," Clayton insisted. "Abby Hamilton has never been anything but trouble."

"But she's an old friend of your sisters'?"

"Yeah."

"I saw all the women—Colleen, the blonde

and the maid of honor—huddled together for a while last night."

Memories flashed through Clayton's mind of all the times he'd found those friends together over the years, the girls and the one nerdy boy who'd hung out with them. "Nothing unusual about that."

"They've been close a long time, huh?"

Clayton nodded. "Yeah."

"Then they know where she is."

"What?" Unable to help himself, he tilted open the blinds again and gazed down the street to where Abby squatted on the grass, her thighs and calves flexing.

"Josh and I are that close," the best man shared. "If he ran off I'd know where he went, even if he didn't tell me." Nick sipped at a cup of coffee.

Clayton should have known where Molly had gone, too. He'd always thought they were close, but now he realized he didn't know his sister at all. He hadn't known face-to-face what Abby had realized in Chicago, that she'd had doubts about her wedding. So Abby probably did know where Molly was. He sighed. "It doesn't matter. She wants to be alone for a while."

Nick shook his head, and his eyes flashed

with emotion. "People shouldn't be alone when they're upset. If I were her brother, I wouldn't care what she'd said in a note. I'd want to see her. Make sure she was okay."

Clayton sighed, torn between following the other man's advice and honoring his sister's wish. Finally, Nick's advice, sound and heartfelt, won the tug-of-war.

And the key to finding Molly was right there, in those short shorts and the little white tank top that revealed a tanned midriff and the tiny waist that his hands had spanned last night when he'd held her close. When he'd kissed her.

"Thank you, Abby, for helping me clean up the mess," Mrs. Hild said.

Abby held tight to the other woman's hand, helping her up from her lawn. Eight years ago she'd thought the woman too old to spend so much time playing in the dirt. Now she understood. Mrs. Hild's roses were like the children she'd never had. "I'm sorry."

"It was those crazy Hendrix boys, not you."

"This time," Abby agreed. "But I've been responsible for tearing up your yard before."

"A long time ago," Mrs. Hild said, "and you always helped me clean up after."

Because Mrs. Hild had insisted she'd press charges if Abby didn't. And so she'd learned her gardening skills from the woman.

"I shouldn't have held you responsible," Mrs. Hild admitted. "Like Mary McClintock reminded me after you left, you didn't have an easy childhood."

She hadn't really had a childhood at all, except when she'd been over at the Mc-Clintocks'. "That's no excuse."

"Ah, honey." Mrs. Hild squeezed Abby's hand. "Come inside for some coffee."

Caffeine was the last thing she needed, especially after last night and Clayton's kiss. His kiss had wound her up more than a double espresso. After talking to her friends, she'd left the crowded reception hall for the security of Mrs. Mick's Dutch Colonial, using it as a refuge just as she had when she was a kid.

Apparently, she'd worried for nothing about anyone having witnessed the kiss. Mrs. Hild hadn't mentioned it, and she was the biggest busybody in Cloverville.

"I'd love to have coffee with you," Abby admitted, still stunned at the woman's change of attitude. But her attitude change wasn't nearly as surprising as Clayton's. He'd gone from hating her to kissing her? "I'll have to join you another time, though. I want to finish my run before Lara wakes up."

"She's a beautiful little girl," the older woman said, squeezing Abby's hand again. "And so well-behaved."

"Yes, she is." Abby's heart expanded, filling with pride. "I'm so lucky."

"You're not lucky," Mrs. Hild protested. "You're a good mother."

"I'd like to take the credit, but I had a lot of help."

"Not from your family," Mrs. Hild surmised.

"No." Abby hadn't seen her mother since she'd left Cloverville, and her father had stopped coming home long before that. After Abby had run away, she'd heard her mother had, too, with a married bartender.

"Lara had a wonderful nanny. Miss Ramsey—a retired schoolteacher." And the woman had mothered Abby as much as she had Lara. "But recently she had to retire from babysitting to take care of her ailing mother in Florida. So she had to leave Chicago."

"You should, too," Mrs. Hild advised, still holding tight to Abby's hand. "You should come home, where family can help you raise your daughter."

"I don't have any family here," Abby reminded the woman. Maybe her memory had begun to slip.

"Honey, *everyone* in Cloverville is family." Despite her age, Mrs. Hild was strong enough to pull Abby into a tight embrace. "You shouldn't have stayed away so long."

Abby blinked hard, fighting back the mist of tears that was threatening to blind her. "I didn't think I'd be welcome," she murmured, ducking her head beneath the wide brim of Mrs. Hild's flower-trimmed straw hat.

"You didn't stick around long enough for tempers to cool and for everyone to settle down. No one was as upset about what happened to the colonel as they were about Mr. McClintock. Emotions were running high just then."

Abby had understood that even at the time. That was why she hadn't taken off until after his funeral. She'd wanted to be there for Molly and Colleen.

Who had been there for Clayton?

"I did fine on my own," Abby insisted. "I lived in some big cities."

"You started your business," Mrs. Hild said with admiration.

"When did you hear about Temps to Go?" Yesterday at the wedding, when she'd answered some of the less personal of those intrusive questions?

"I've known for a little while now. Mary McClintock brags about you like you're one of her brood."

If the town busybody had known about her business for a while, how come Clayton didn't know? Was he so uninterested in her that he'd never listened to anything anyone had said about her?

"Mary says that you put yourself through school," Mrs. Hild continued. "And that your business is doing very well."

Abby listened for the disbelief, for the doubt that she'd managed not only to get an education, but also to launch a successful business. But the other woman only smiled— Mrs. Mick must have done a lot of talking in order to change Mrs. Hild's opinion.

"Most temp agencies specialize in either office or manufacturing personnel. But temporary workers are needed in many fields beyond those two." Fortunately. She'd worked any job she'd been able to find to support herself when she'd first left Cloverville. Sick of pounding the pavement to find those jobs, she'd put an ad in the paper listing the skills she'd accumulated while growing up. The Kellys had taught her to cook and bake. And Mrs. Mick had taught her to sew and clean, as well as raise children. Once she'd placed the ad, she began to receive calls from both potential employers and people who shared her skills and wanted employment. Thus, her business was launched, for the price of a classified ad, in a run-down motel room in Detroit. "I have a lot of retired people on my staff, who just want to work part-time and have myriad skills to offer."

"We could use an office here," Mrs. Hild continued, "with all the new businesses opening up. Did you notice on your way in from the airport that the place your folks rented had been knocked down for a strip mall?"

She shook her head. Abby hadn't noticed. Of course, she hadn't looked for the shabby bungalow—she'd spent as little time as possible there when she'd lived in Cloverville. And she wanted to forget that.

"I wouldn't mind some help in my garden from time to time," the older woman admitted, "and I know that stubborn Mr. Carpenter could use some help in his store."

"I'm sure I could find workers in this area with many skills."

Mrs. Hild nodded. "Plenty of retired husbands in this town driving their wives crazy."

Abby smiled. "I have a lot of retired husbands *and* wives working for me."

Temps to Go had earned its reputation for being able to fill every need. Why hadn't its success filled all of Abby's needs? She'd proven she wasn't the screwup everyone had considered her to be. She had a beautiful daughter, but sometimes she felt just the same as she had when she'd been growing up in Cloverville, and she yearned for more.

"You really should move back here and open an office."

Although she smiled to soften her refusal, Abby shook her head at the older woman. "I'm not staying. I only came for Molly's wedding."

A gentle hiss escaped the older woman, like steam from an iron. "The wedding that wasn't."

Now she knew who'd coined that particular phrase.

"Poor Molly." Mrs. Hild *tsk*ed her concern. "Do you know where she could be?"

Abby wasn't about to share her suspicions. Instead she pumped her arms and lifted her knees, beginning to jog in place. "I better get back to Mrs. Mick's. I don't want Lara to wake up in a strange place without me."

"See, honey, like I said, you are a good mother."

"Thank you." Her education, the business… Nothing meant as much to her as her daughter. Lara was the best thing Abby had ever done.

"Think about moving back to Cloverville, Abby. It would be a great place to raise your daughter—much safer than a big city."

"I'll think about it," she said as she plugged her earphones back in.

Abby swiped a hand across her eyes, wondering if they burned because of perspiration. But she hadn't run long or hard enough to work up a sweat. Yet. She would sprint back to the McClintock house. Waving goodbye to Mrs. Hild, she headed down Main Street at a jog, admiring the gleam in the windows of Mr. Carpenter's hardware store.

He needed help? Somehow she doubted that, but she knew from the others she'd talked to at the reception that the town actually did have a need for her business. Brenna could use more help at the bakery, which she'd expanded since taking over for her parents.

Abby inhaled the fragrance of baking bread and cinnamon rolls. Her stomach grumbled. Maybe she'd pick up some rolls before she headed back to Mrs. Mick's. Not that she needed any sugar.

She blinked again as she neared McClintock Insurance. She could remember, as a little girl, coming to the office with Molly and Colleen, how Mr. McClintock had always handed out candy. He'd had such a sweet tooth and had been such a kind man. Losing him had left a hole not only in the McClintock family but in the rest of Cloverville, too.

From everyone singing his praises at the reception the night before, she'd learned that Clayton had done his best to fill that void with his family and with the town. Had assuming his father's responsibilities filled the hole his dad's passing had undoubtedly left in Clayton's life?

Who had taken care of *him* eight years ago? Did he ever yearn, as Abby did, for something he couldn't quite name?

Her feet slowed as she paused outside the

office next to the insurance agency, her attention drawn to a For Lease sign. The space was large enough for a branch office of Temps to Go. Maybe it was even large enough for the headquarters.

She'd kept her promise to Mrs. Hild, after all. But how could she even consider moving back to Cloverville? Because maybe Mrs. Hild was right and it would be a great, safe place to raise her daughter. Abby would make any sacrifice for Lara.

Did she dare ask Clayton about leasing the office?

No. She shook her head to clear the crazy idea from her mind. Then she geared up, ready to sprint. But before she could do more than draw a deep breath, an arm wrapped around her shoulders, pulling her back into the alley between buildings.

Cloverville safe? Yeah, right. She didn't bother screaming. No one was awake this early to hear her but Mrs. Hild, and she didn't want to scare the old woman into a heart attack.

Ignoring the mad pounding of her heart, Abby slammed her elbow into a hard stomach, stomped on her assailant's instep and then whirled, with her knee lifted. Her actions being trained reflexes learned in self-defense courses, she couldn't stop herself even though she recognized her assailant… right before she connected with her knee and dropped him onto the pavement.

Chapter Seven

Doubled over on the asphalt, Clayton groaned and gasped for breath. He hadn't wanted to scare Abby but, plugged into her music, she hadn't heard him call out to her. When he'd caught her in his arms, he hadn't expected he'd be left writhing in the alley. God, he hurt.

"Clayton!" she shouted. "You shouldn't have grabbed me."

Wincing at the volume of her voice, he gestured toward his ears so she'd think to remove her earphones.

"Did you hit your head?" she asked, dropping beside him. She ran her fingers through his hair, as if checking for bumps.

His scalp tingled from her gentle touch. "Are you okay?"

Pride had him nodding, even though he was in major pain. Good thing Nick had already left the apartment—he wouldn't have wanted another guy to see him like this, nearly curled up in the fetal position. He hated Abby seeing him like this. He sucked in a ragged breath, trying to be a man. If that was even possible after being kneed. He reached out and pulled the wires from her headphones.

"You can stop yelling. I'm not deaf." *Paralyzed, maybe.* "I called out to you, but you started running away."

"Clayton, I'm so sorry. I didn't hear you." Her cheeks flushed pink and her eyes grew soft with regret. But then they flashed again with anger. "You shouldn't have grabbed me, though."

He bit back a groan as he shifted on the ground. "I wanted to talk to you."

"And now you want to wring my neck again?" she asked, a hint of amusement in her voice.

"I know better than to mess with you," he said. For a petite woman, she sure packed a wallop.

"Most men do," she declared, leaning down to offer him her hand.

He narrowed his eyes as he stared up at her, still doubled over. Then he waved off her hand and, with a grunt and a grimace, lurched to his feet. "Now I know how you survived when you took off on your own to the big city."

"I've been taking care of myself for a long time," she agreed. But she didn't have only herself to think about anymore; she had Lara. She needed to get back to Mrs. Mick's, but she couldn't leave Clayton until she knew he was really okay. He couldn't even stand up straight yet. Dirt smeared the white T-shirt he wore with faded jeans that rode low on his lean hips.

"Let me help you upstairs," she said, turning toward the stairwell that wound up the outside of his building.

The tight line of Clayton's mouth lifted into a slight grin. "I've been taking care of myself for a long time, too."

Himself or just everyone else? Abby wanted to ask him, but maybe it was better that she didn't learn any more about Clayton McClintock. Knowing how he kissed had kept her awake all night.

"I crippled you," she said. "Let me help." She eased close to his side and wound her arm around his back. Muscles rippled beneath her touch as Clayton tensed. She inhaled the scent of his citrusy aftershave.

"I'm not quite crippled," he said, as he maneuvered up the first step without leaning on her at all. "Maybe emasculated, though."

"Emasculated?" she repeated, strangling on a laugh. Even as a boy, Clayton McClintock had been all man, all testosterone and an overdeveloped sense of responsibility, trying to take care of everyone even before his dad had gotten sick. Of course, at the time, she'd considered his behavior bossy and manipulative.

"Like you haven't emasculated a guy before," he groused.

The laugh she'd struggled to contain finally slipped out. "Yes, but usually only after I've dated them."

A chuckle rumbled in Clayton's chest, then he winced and some of his weight and warmth settled on her. "Don't make me laugh."

What amused him? The thought of her dating anyone else—or her dating *him?*

Her skin tingled and heated. She gazed up into his face, so close to hers. And she thought again of the night before, of the kiss he'd stolen in the middle of the reception hall.

She closed her eyes as sensations rushed over her; she could almost taste him again. He'd tasted like champagne, dry and expensive and certain to make her lose control. It was why Abby didn't drink. With her ADD, she'd had enough of a struggle gaining control of her life and she couldn't afford to lose it, for anyone.

As she stumbled on the steps, Abby opened her eyes. Clayton supported her now, holding her steady so she wouldn't fall down.

"Well, you're fine," she said. In those old jeans and the smudged T-shirt that hugged every muscle of his long, lean body, he was much too fine for Abby's peace of mind. "I should go."

His hand wrapped around her arm, his fingers sliding over her bare skin. "Come inside for a while. We need to talk."

"Don't worry about it," she said as he ushered her through the door to his apartment. "I know it was nothing."

"What was nothing?" he asked as he closed the door behind them, shutting them inside his sun-drenched kitchen.

Abby gazed around the room, impressed

with the antique cabinets, some of them polished oak and others painted deep burgundy and slate blue. Hardwood floors had been stripped and polished, as well, while the exterior walls remained bare, red brick. She grabbed a dish towel, then walked over to the fridge to fill it with ice from the dispenser.

"Abby!" Clayton shouted above the grinding of the ice machine. "*What* was nothing?"

Abby walked over to where he leaned against the marble counter. "Last night. The kiss." She reached toward his waist with her makeshift ice pack.

Clayton caught her wrist, his long fingers wrapping around her leaping pulse. "Just where are you thinking about putting that?"

"You're such a prude, Clayton," she teased, her eyes alight with a mischievous twinkle as she reached for the hem of his T-shirt. When she pushed the cotton above his stomach, her breath hissed out between her teeth.

He glanced down to see if she'd done as much damage with her elbow as she had with her knee, but she'd only marked him with an uneven red circle on his rib cage. "It's nothing," he assured her. Nothing, just like their kiss had been nothing. "It probably won't even bruise."

She pressed the ice-filled towel to the red mark. "You... You need to..."

"I don't need ice," he gasped as the cold, wet towel stuck to his skin. "I'm fine, really."

"Mm-mmmm..."

"Abby?" Although he called her name, she didn't look up, her attention focused on his bare chest and abdomen. She wasn't as uninterested in his boring self as she'd like him to believe. He covered her hand on the towel, pulling the ice away. "I don't need this," he said as he tossed the makeshift ice pack into the sink, the cubes clinking against the stainless steel surface.

"Lara doesn't like ice packs, either," she murmured.

"So what do you do to make her feel better?"

"I kiss..." Her face flushed red, and she pulled her gaze from his chest to meet his eyes.

Clayton's body hardened, the pain she'd inflicted forgotten as desire flared to life. She hadn't killed him, but getting involved with her would probably make him wish he were dead. He didn't need her kind of trouble in his life. But he couldn't stop himself from goading her. "Then, where's my kiss?"

Her eyes widened. "Clayton!"

"If kissing me is nothing..."

"Last night," she said, then licked her lips. "It was the wedding."

"There was no wedding."

"The wedding that wasn't," she murmured.

He sighed. No doubt Cloverville would forever refer to it as that. "The bride ran off. I haven't forgotten that you had something to do with that."

"Did you really want Molly to marry a man she doesn't love?"

"I want to talk to Molly. I want to make sure that you're not the reason she's confused, that you didn't talk her out of something she wanted to do."

"Clayton!" She should have known better than to think he'd forgiven her part in Molly's running away. Clayton would never let her forget anything she did. Including the kiss.

"But most importantly," he said, his voice deep with emotion, "I want to make sure she's all right."

Her irritation faded and her heart swelled in sympathy. He loved his sister. "She is all right."

"So she did tell you in the note. You know where she is."

"No, I don't." Not for certain, at least, but she had a suspicion. If she told Clayton that Eric South probably had a houseguest, he would charge over there this minute and insist on talking to Molly. Abby had to honor her friend's request for time because she wasn't sure she could honor her other request. Just how long could she stay in Cloverville? While apparently the town had accepted that she'd changed, being back here made *her* feel as if she hadn't. She felt like that unloved, out-of-control girl all over again. And no one made her feel as out of control and as inadequate as Clayton McClintock.

"Abby, don't lie to me."

"Clayton, you're never going to trust me." Of course she'd given him a few reasons to be that way, back in her rebellious youth. The tattoos—he hadn't made it to the parlor in time to stop Molly and Colleen from getting theirs. "You'll never believe that I'm telling you the truth."

"Why should I?"

"I've never lied to you." Not really. Only by omission.

"Yes, you have," he insisted.

Okay, he was more intuitive than she'd realized. "When have I lied to you?"

"When you told me that it was nothing."

"What was nothing?" she asked, even though she already knew the answer. Her heart pounded hard as she tried to figure out why it mattered so much to him that she'd dismissed their kiss. Male pride?

"Our kiss," he said. "Last night."

"You kissed *me,*" she reminded him, pride lifting her chin and preventing her from asking him why he had. She'd probably been asking for it. With her eyes, with the way she'd melted in his arms. She'd wondered for so long what it would feel like for Clayton Mc-Clintock to kiss her.

"And you kissed me back," he said.

"Clayton McClintock, ever the gentleman."

He reached for her again, but not as he had on the deserted sidewalk. He slid one arm around her waist and his other hand cupped the back of her head, his fingers tangling in her ponytail. Then he brought her mouth to his. His lips touched hers with heat and passion.

Abby's heart raced in her chest as her pulse throbbed. She clenched her hands into fists so that she wouldn't reach for him. So that she wouldn't kiss him back. But she closed her eyes and an image swam into her mind—his chest bared to her hungry gaze. His well-developed muscles dusted with hair that arrowed down over the ripples of his washboard stomach to the low-riding waist of his worn jeans. She'd wanted to kiss his bruise, but she'd resisted. Then.

His tongue slipped between her lips, teasing hers. She couldn't suppress a moan as the pleasure spread, like hot fudge over ice cream, through her body. Melting her resistance, all her instincts for self-preservation. She couldn't remember the last time a man had kissed her in this way. Maybe never. Certainly, she had never been so weak-kneed, so dizzy with desire.

As her world tilted, Abby reached out to stop herself from falling. She clutched Clayton's shoulders, her fingers digging into the sinewy muscles just beneath the thin cotton fabric.

"Clayton," she whispered, moving her mouth on his, allowing him to deepen their kiss. Even though her skin heated with passion, she shivered.

His hands, wide-palmed and long-fingered, skimmed over her back and down to her hips. He pulled her closer. So close she had proof that she definitely hadn't emasculated him.

Clayton groaned, in a different kind of pain.

Because of Abby Hamilton. His hands molded themselves to the curve of her hips as he fought the urge to lift her against him and carry her off to his bedroom. Instead, he pulled her away. But the distance didn't cool the fire raging through his veins, burning up his common sense.

"You don't feel better," she murmured as she stumbled back a few steps. Her face flushed, her eyes glittered with desire.

She wanted him, too.

He groaned again, fighting the urge to reach for her, to drag her back in his arms, back against his hard, aching body. "What?"

"You got your kiss," she pointed out, "but you're not feeling any better."

"No, I'm not," he admitted. In fact, he felt a hell of a lot worse. Abby Hamilton? What the hell was he thinking? Maybe all the McClintocks were losing their minds. Rory was sneaking alcohol. Molly had run out on her wedding. And *he* was making out with Abby Hamilton.

"Maybe I did hit my head in the alley," he muttered, rubbing a hand over his face. He couldn't look at her, not without wanting her.

"And what about last night? What's your excuse for kissing me then?" she asked.

A warning bell clanged in Clayton's head,

but he chose to ignore it. "Too much champagne."

"So you'd have to be drunk or suffering a concussion to want to kiss me?" she asked, sparks in her eyes as she glared at him. "Thanks a lot!"

"Abby…"

"You're not arguing with me," she pointed out.

"You're beautiful," he said. "You know you are."

But beauty had never meant much to Clayton. She knew that. "You still think I'm a flake, huh? Or an idiot. Oh, that's right. You don't think I'm *smart* enough for you." All her childhood insecurities came rushing back, dousing the desire she'd felt. Anger consumed her now. She had to get out of this town and away from this man.

"Abby…"

"Because I got expelled, you think I never finished school," she accused him. "But I did. I went to college, too. I took business courses."

"That's great," he praised.

Maybe he was sincere, but Abby sensed condescension, if only in her own head.

"I know school was hard for you," he continued.

"I didn't get a degree," she admitted. "I didn't have time." Not with launching her business, then becoming a single mother.

"And you probably lost interest before you finished," he guessed. "Nothing ever kept your interest for long. That's probably why you move around so much, why you work temp jobs."

"*Work* temp jobs?" She'd suspected he hadn't known about her business, and now she had proof. "You think that's all I do?"

"Abby, there's nothing wrong with that. You're obviously supporting yourself and Lara. You've always been a hard worker."

"Wow, did that hurt?" she asked. "Actually saying something nice about me?"

"Abby…"

"So you heard about Temps to Go and just assumed I work for the place?"

His eyes narrowed as his gaze met hers.

"Well, you know what they say about assumptions and the people who make them. I *own* the business, Clayton. I didn't inherit it or buy someone out. I built it from the ground up." And she was damned proud of the little business she'd launched with one ad in the classifieds. "I'm not the stupid girl who got expelled from high school anymore."

"You didn't get expelled over your grades," Clayton pointed out, "and I never said you were stupid."

"Yes, you did. Eight years ago," she reminded him. *Stupid* was one of the nicer names he'd called her after he'd assumed that she'd driven her car into the statue of Colonel Clover.

"You accuse me of not being able to let go of the past," he said. "But it seems I'm not the only one."

"No, you're not," she admitted. "That's why I can't stay." In his apartment or in Cloverville. Molly had asked too much of her.

As she headed for the door, he didn't try to stop her. He didn't reach for her as she passed him, either. He let her walk away. Just as he had eight years ago. Abby slammed the door shut on him, on the crazy attraction she'd felt for him.

Nothing could come of her desire for Clayton McClintock, because even though he might want her, he would never respect her.

"I wish you'd stay in Cloverville."

Abby closed her eyes, holding back her

tears. The request didn't come from the Mc-
Clintock she wished would ask her to stay.
She shook her head, disgusted with herself
for wanting a man who didn't really want her,
and she forced a smile for Mrs. Mick, who sat
on the edge of the bed in Clayton's old room.

With tan walls and plush carpet, Mrs. Mick
had achieved the look and comfort of an upscale hotel room. From her travels between
offices, Abby was quite familiar with hotel
rooms. She had one booked in Raleigh, North
Carolina, right now, to check out the city as
the possible location for the headquarters of
Temps to Go and a home for her and Lara.
She'd always heard that people in the South
were as warm as their weather.

Her eyes filled with sadness, Mrs. Mc-
Clintock watched Abby fold clothes back into
her open suitcase. "You should really stay."

Abby's heart twisted, and she fought
against the emotion welling in her throat.
Mrs. Mick hadn't wanted her to leave eight
years ago, either. She'd wanted her to move
in with them, but Abby had intruded enough
on the McClintock family during their time
of inconsolable grief. "I can't…"

"You can. You've proven you can do anything you want to do," her champion insisted.

Abby's heart swelled. How she wished this woman had been her mother. "You're going to make me cry," she said, biting her lip to retain her self-control.

"Good, then we'll both have a good cry."

"What is that?" Abby asked, perplexed by the phrase she'd heard often but had never really understood. "A *good* cry?"

"Didn't you cry when Lara was born?" Mrs. Mick knew the answer to her question, since she'd insisted on coming east to Detroit for the delivery.

"Yes, I cried when Lara was born," she reminded the older woman. "But I was in pain." And terrified she would fail the precious baby who was dependent solely on her.

"And you were happy."

She'd brought a beautiful angel into the world, and she had had the most important people in her life with her, supporting her. As Mrs. Hild had pointed out, she'd had *her family*.

"So, that's a good cry," Abby said, understanding the older woman's point.

"Yes, just as people cry at weddings."

"There were some people crying last night," Abby acknowledged.

Mrs. McClintock smiled. "Just Clayton, when he was writing checks."

Abby couldn't suppress a smile of her own, but she refused to comment on Clayton. She didn't want to think about him, either; she'd thought about him enough last night while she'd lain awake reliving their kiss. "Have you heard from her?"

"Molly?" the runaway bride's mother asked, concern tensing her face before she relaxed with obvious faith in her oldest daughter.

Abby nodded. "Molly."

"No, I haven't heard from her," she admitted with a heavy sigh. "You should stay until we do."

That had been Abby's intention until her most recent run-in with the bride's brother. Molly would understand.

Mrs. McClintock persisted. "She's going to need her friends when she comes home."

Abby hated to worry the older woman, but she had to raise the question. "What makes you so sure, once Molly sorts out what she really wants, that she'll come home?"

"All my children come home. Clayton, from college…"

Because his father had gotten sick, he'd foregone dorm and fraternity parties to return every weekend. But then maybe he'd also come back more to make sure Abby hadn't badly influenced his sisters than to take care of his dad.

"And Molly came home from college and now from med school. Colleen and Rory have never left."

Colleen out of guilt. Abby held in a sigh of concern for her young friend.

Mrs. McClintock beamed. "And you came home, too."

Abby blinked hard. "I'm not one of your children." Not that she hadn't wished a hundred times during her childhood that she was.

Mrs. Mick rose from the bed and pulled Abby into a tight embrace. "Of course you're one of my children, Abby Hamilton. I raised you just like I raised my own."

"I don't think I've ever told you how much I appreciate everything you've done for me," Abby realized. She didn't know if Mrs. Mick even understood how much she'd done, how much she'd meant to Abby. If not for Mrs. Mick's example, she wouldn't have known how to be a mother.

"You showed me," the older woman assured her. "When you lived in Cloverville, you made me such beautiful gifts."

The school craft projects, which she was supposed to bring her mother for Mother's Day and Christmas, she'd given to Mrs. Mick instead. Her parents would only have used them as weapons when her dad came home from the road and confronted her mom over her latest drunken affair.

The other woman smiled with affection. "You picked me flowers...?"

"Mrs. Hild didn't appreciate that, though."

Her adopted mother laughed. "No, she didn't. I had to hide them when she came over to gab."

"Sorry."

"Your heart was in the right place," Mrs. McClintock said, defending her. "And even after you left, you sent me cards and called. You're one of my kids, Abby."

She appreciated the sentiment, but she'd always known she wasn't a true McClintock. Clayton had made certain she hadn't ever believed she was one of them.

"So like I do to my kids," she continued, "I'm going to give you some unsolicited advice."

Mrs. Mick enjoyed painting herself as a meddling mother, but she wasn't the real meddler of the McClintocks. The role of primary manipulator belonged to her oldest child, the man who always had to be in control. Yet when he'd kissed her in the middle of the crowded dance floor and then again in his apartment, it hadn't felt as if he was in control.

"I would happily pay for your advice," Abby insisted. She needed it now more than she ever had.

"I'd like to work for you," Mrs. McClintock admitted. "Since there's only Rory, I'm not as busy as I'd like to be. I think it would be fun to be a temp, to work different jobs, to have some variety in my life."

Clayton was nothing like his mother. He seemed to like everything the way it was, under his control. That was why he'd never want Abby as part of his life.

"You'd make a great temp," Abby said.

"Then open a branch of Temps to Go here. With the way Cloverville is growing and its proximity to Grand Rapids, you'd have a thriving business in no time."

The idea had appealed to her, but she shook her head. "No."

"Think about it," Mrs. McClintock implored her. "I even have the ideal office space for you. Right next to the McClintock Insurance Agency."

Maybe she was more of a meddler than Abby

had liked to think. Was it just a coincidence that the space was still open? Or was this another ploy, like Clayton picking her up at the airport, to throw the two of them together? Was Mrs. Mick also behind Molly's request that Abby stay in town?

She shrugged off the notion. Mrs. Mick wasn't that devious. And Abby *had* considered the empty office in Clayton's building to be an ideal space. "I don't think I could get along with the landlord, though." Without killing him.

Mrs. McClintock shook her head. "Give Clayton time. He just has to get used to Abby Hamilton being grown up."

"I have a daughter. I'm a businesswoman." And still, he didn't respect her.

"You have to give him time to absorb all that."

That was why she'd sprinted home to pack. She didn't want to give him time, but even more than giving him time, she didn't want to give herself time to fall for him.

Abby shook her head. "I can't stay in Cloverville."

Mrs. McClintock lifted the clothes from the suitcase and put them back in the open dresser drawers. "Yes, you can, Abby. You're home. You just need time to accept that."

Because she loved the older woman, she couldn't argue with her. Not now. She would wait until they heard from Molly, and then she'd pack up and head the hell out of Cloverville as quickly as she'd run away once before.

Chapter Eight

"She's on the phone." The screen door hadn't even shut behind Clayton before his mother made the announcement.

"Molly's on the phone?" he asked as he joined her in the big country kitchen where his family had spent so much of their lives.

Focusing on the dishes in the sink, she shook her head. "Abby. Isn't that who you've come to see?"

"Why would you assume that?" he asked. Who, besides the best man, had witnessed their kiss on the dance floor?

"Defensive, much?" Rory goaded him as he galloped through the kitchen doorway with a giggling Lara on his back, her arms wound so tight around his neck that his voice was a bit strangled.

Lucky kid. Clayton couldn't count the number of times he'd been tempted to choke the teenager.

His mom reached for the little girl, but Rory charged around the kitchen island, avoiding her. "Rory! Don't go shaking up Lara. She just ate."

"We ate a while ago," Rory argued. Rory always argued. "I know because I'm hungry already."

"You're always hungry," his mother countered, shaking her head as an affectionate twinkle crept into her eyes. Rory was her baby, and she always caved and spoiled him rotten. Maybe Clayton needed to tell her just how much trouble her *baby* had gotten into lately. But he hated to worry her—she'd done so *much* worrying.

"He's the one she's going to get sick on," Clayton pointed out to his mother. "Lara, you have to kick him like you would a horse, to get him to go faster."

The child stared at him with curious eyes.

"You know, pretend you have spurs like the cowboys do." If she were half as strong as her mother, she'd probably have Rory writhing on the kitchen floor. His brother took off again, before his rider could spur him to go faster.

"Clayton!" His mother's voice rose as she swatted his shoulder with a dish towel. "I'm sure Abby doesn't want her daughter getting sick."

"So Abby's on the phone?" he asked. "You're sure she's not talking to Molly?"

"I hope not."

"Mom!" Her reaction floored him. His mother had seemed to take in stride Molly running out on her wedding. He'd never suspected she was as angry as he'd been. Of course, he'd been madder at Abby than Molly.

"I want to hear from my daughter," his mother assured him. "But the minute we know Molly's fine, Abby will be leaving us." She sighed. "She was going to leave this afternoon."

After their kiss.

"But I talked her into staying. Of course, she might have changed her mind again. For all I know, she's on the phone with the airport."

Clayton's stomach clenched, as if someone had driven spurs into him. Not that he should be surprised. He knew how much Abby hated

Cloverville. She'd only come home for Molly's wedding, to talk Molly out of marrying her groom. He waited for his anger to return, but nothing happened. He'd rather have paid for a welcome home party for Abby than a wedding for Molly, if his sister was going to be miserable in the marriage.

"Where is she?" If she was using her cell phone, she might not even be in the house.

"In your father's den."

His stomach clenched even tighter. He hadn't been in that paneled room since his father died. The den was *where* his father had died. Too weak to climb stairs to his bedroom on the second floor, his father had spent the last days of his life in a hospital bed in his den, slowly and painfully dying. Clayton couldn't go in there, not even to talk to Abby.

"So you don't know who she's talking to?" he persisted.

His mother shrugged. "I had her use the den, so she'd have some privacy. She said she had some calls to make. I didn't pry to find out who she was calling, but I know it's not a boyfriend. She's single—like you."

But Abby wasn't single. She had Lara, who rode in again on his brother's back. But this time she wasn't giggling. "You bummed her out," Rory accused Clayton. "Now she's worried about cowboys kicking horses."

"They don't hurt them," Clayton insisted as he reached out for the little girl. She unwound her arms from around Rory's neck and put a hand on Clayton's shoulder as he held her. Her blue eyes were serious as she stared into his face.

"Aren't spurs sharp?" she asked.

"Good going," Rory murmured as he opened the refrigerator door and peered inside at the contents.

His young brother was right. He also had two softhearted sisters, and he should have known better than to mention any possibility of an animal being harmed.

"The spurs don't hurt the horses," he said, although he had no way of knowing for certain if that was true. He was hardly a cowboy. Maybe if he were, he'd be more like Abby's type. Yet, she'd insisted she didn't go for the type he'd suspected. He doubted she'd spoken the truth when she'd confessed to going for *his* type—she'd only been teasing him, as she always had.

But she had kissed him back.

The kiss, *kisses,* hadn't meant anything, though. To either of them. Last night he'd succumbed to temptation and today to aggravation. Abby Hamilton never failed to aggravate him. Even now, while she used his father's den. He hated the thought of anyone but his father making use of that room.

"You promise?" Lara asked, gazing up at him through her long, thick lashes.

His heart skipped a beat, she looked so much like her mother. He leaned his forehead against hers and assured her, "Horses are tough."

"Not this horse," Rory griped as he swung the refrigerator door shut. "This horse is tired and hungry. Mom, there's nothing to eat. I'm going to walk into town and get some ice cream."

"You're grounded," Clayton reminded his brother. He should have grounded him for life over the spiked punch, especially after he'd heard a few other people had gotten glasses of it before the bartender had dumped out the bowl.

Instead of sputtering that Clayton wasn't his father, Rory shrugged and walked out of the kitchen. Lara wriggled down from Clayton's arms and skipped out after her "horse."

His mother turned on Clayton, using the

very words Rory had refrained from shouting this time. "You're not his father."

Coming from her, the words hurt even more than when Rory hurled them. "Mom?"

"You're taking on too much responsibility—just like your father was afraid you would."

Clayton stepped back, staggered by his mother's comment. He'd never known his dad had worried about him.

His mom's eyes softened sympathetically. "That's why he insisted you finish college."

Clayton had wanted to drop out when his father was diagnosed with cancer. But his dad hadn't allowed him to come home then. He'd forced him to stay in school.

"None of that has anything to do with Rory." Clayton shouldn't have kept his younger brother's misdeeds from their mother. "I haven't told you what he's been getting into."

"I know."

"You do?" Had he underestimated his mother, just as he'd underestimated Abby?

"Cloverville's a small town. I've talked to the neighbors and I've talked to his teachers."

"One teacher in particular?" he asked. "Mr. Schipper?"

His mother's face flushed and she patted her hair with a trembling hand. "Maybe."

"Mom, it's okay if you want to start going out."

"I know," she interrupted him. "I don't need my kids' permission to start dating."

But maybe she thought she needed her dead husband's permission. "Mom, if you ever want to talk, you know I'm here for you. Right?"

"We're talking about Rory."

"So what are you going to do?" he asked, accepting the fact that she was primarily responsible for her youngest child. Not that Clayton wouldn't help her.

"I was thinking about military school."

Clayton rolled his head back again, shocked.

"But then Abby talked to him."

"What?" He'd realized he was losing control over Rory, but he had wanted to handle his brother without upsetting his mother—and especially without involving Abby Hamilton.

"And he apologized."

Clayton laughed, amused by how easily his brother charmed their mother. "C'mon, Mom. Rory knows how to work you."

She shook her head. "He was sincere. He promised he'd stop hanging around the Hendrix boys."

He opened his mouth, then shut it, holding in his doubts about Abby's ability to influence Rory and the teenager's promises to behave. "So you're letting him off the hook?"

She nodded. "Until he screws up again."

"Then it's military school?"

"That's what *he* thinks," she said, smiling. Then she called out for the teenager. Instead of taking his usual sweet time to answer his mother, Rory trotted back into the room, Lara riding his back again. "If you wait until Abby gets off the phone," she told him, "we can all walk to town together. Lara, would you like some ice cream?"

"Yes, please," the child said, perfectly polite.

"Clayton, do you want to join us?"

"For ice cream?"

"Yes."

"Hey, why did you stop by tonight?" Rory asked, his face tensing as if he feared punishment for some crime for which Clayton had yet to catch him. Instead of avoiding his older brother, however, Rory walked closer to him, meeting his gaze head-on.

Clayton wasn't sure why he'd come over to his mom's tonight. He'd simply been drawn to the house, to Abby, for some reason. Probably because once again he needed to apologize to her for misjudging her. Maybe he *was* as judgmental as she'd accused him of being.

"Don't you like ice cream?" Lara asked incredulously.

"I like ice cream," he admitted. In fact, since he'd kissed Abby at the wedding, he'd developed quite a craving for sweets. But that wasn't why he'd stopped by. He had no intention of kissing her ever again. They brought out the worst in each other.

"I think he stopped by to talk to your mama," his mother teased.

Catching the matchmaking gleam in his mom's dark eyes, Clayton shook his head. "No. Not at all."

Lara's small hand patted his cheek, turning his attention back to her. "Don't you like my mommy?"

A while ago he might not have spared the child's feelings and answered with a quick and unequivocal no. But now that he'd gotten to know Abby Hamilton—not the rebellious teen but the accomplished woman—he couldn't answer that question, not without lying to himself.

His mother, staring at him as intently as

Lara did, chuckled. "I think he likes your mother a lot, sweetie."

Lara leaned around Rory's shoulder and pressed her mouth to Clayton's cheek. "Good. Because I like you, Clayton." But she wouldn't have admitted her feelings if he didn't like her mother. Smart and loyal. While, before, he'd wondered how Abby had raised a child such as this, now he was beginning to understand. The little girl hadn't just inherited her mother's looks.

"You like me even though I didn't find the bride for you?" he teased.

Letting go of Rory, she wrapped an arm around Clayton's neck and hugged him. "You tried."

If only her mother were that forgiving.

"I like you, too, sweetheart," he said.

"Here," his mom said, pulling the little girl off Rory's back. "Let's visit the bathroom before we head out for our walk. Clayton, why don't you look in on Abby and see if she's done with her calls yet."

"Subtle," Clayton murmured as he watched Lara and his mother disappear from the kitchen.

"Don't worry about Mom trying to match you up with Abby. Everyone knows she's too cool for *you,*" Rory said. His bright eyes gleamed with a hint of lust. "Not to mention way too hot."

For once Clayton couldn't argue with his kid brother. Well, not about Abby. Apparently, she *had* had an effect on the hormonal teenager, just not the one his mother believed. "Hey, I've dated plenty of hot women."

Rory snorted. "Yeah, right. You date old chicks."

"Old?"

"Yeah, you know, your age." Rory grimaced as if totally disgusted—like he'd drunk half a gallon of milk before noticing it had gone sour. "And boring."

"Responsible." That had been one of his first dating rules. He only dated responsible, independent women, so maybe they tended to be his age or older. He hadn't been looking for anything serious or lasting, but he hadn't wanted a mess, either, which might have resulted from dating someone immature or romantically optimistic.

"And Abby isn't that much younger than I am." Only four years.

Rory pushed his curly hair out of his eyes, as if he needed to see Clayton clearer, and then he shook his head. "You've been old as long as I remember."

Maybe he had been. Clayton sighed with resignation.

"It's okay. I get why," Rory said. Then, in a sincere tone, he added, *"Thanks."*

Clayton lifted his chin, almost as if his brother had slugged him. He reeled at Rory's change of attitude. "What?"

"For stepping in." The boy's throat moved as he swallowed hard. "For Dad. You took care of stuff. I get that now."

What the hell had Abby said to him?

"You're a pain in the ass sometimes, but I understand why," Rory said, nodding as if in approval. "I know I've been one, too, lately. I'm sorry."

Clayton resisted the urge to make him repeat his apology, but he didn't need to hear it again to realize his brother meant what he said. The boy's eyes were damp with regret. "You're a good kid."

Despite the hint of tears, Rory grinned. "No, I'm not. But I will be. People change."

Like Abby Hamilton had. "Yeah, people do."

"Abby isn't much older than me," Rory continued as if he'd never apologized. "She's got the rep for being a rebel. Think she'd mind that I'm jailbait?"

Exasperated but amused, Clayton laughed out loud. "I think she'll mind."

Rory raised his eyebrows dramatically. "Maybe she'll wait for me."

"We're ready," Lara said as she skipped back into the room. "Can we go now?"

"Did you check with Abby, to see if she's done on the phone?" his mom asked.

Clayton shook his head. "No, but go ahead. I'll tell Abby where you went."

Rory narrowed his eyes and leaned close to Clayton to whisper menacingly, "So you want to be alone with her? Don't try to make time with my woman, big brother."

Obviously Rory hadn't seen the kiss at the reception.

"We should probably wait," his mom said. "I don't want to take Lara to town without Abby's permission." She was aware of Abby's antipathy toward Cloverville.

"I'm sure she won't mind," Clayton insisted. And his brother was right. He did want to be alone with her, no matter how dangerous that had proved. Hell, it hadn't mattered when they'd been in the middle of a crowded dance floor. He hadn't been able to control himself then.

But he would now. He had to. Since marriage and fatherhood were not in his plan, he had to resist Abby for her sake, for his sake, and most especially for Lara's sake. The last thing he wanted was to hurt her.

Abby hung up the phone, then pressed a hand against her sore ear. She needed to set up a proper office and bring in some extra help. Checking in with the managers from her Detroit and Chicago offices took too long and kept her away from Lara. She needed a nanny, too. Someone who'd care for her little girl the way Miss Ramsey had in Chicago. She pulled her hand from her aching ear, the throbbing continuing in the back of her eyes, and pushed herself up from Mr. Mick's desk.

Memories of his final days ran through her mind, in this room, his body, once so big and strong, wasting away in a hospital bed. Despite the pain he'd suffered, he'd kept his cheerful, loving demeanor until the very end.

No matter how much Clayton had resented her presence, every other McClintock had welcomed her as a member of the family. And no one more than Mr. Mick. She blinked hard, clearing the teary mist from her eyes. The room hadn't changed. Knotty pine paneling still lined the walls. The same beige commercial carpet covered the floor. Only the hospital bed was gone. His old metal desk and low-backed leather davenport sat where they always had.

Unnerved by the sudden quiet in the room, which was echoed by an eerie silence emanating from the rest of the house, Abby scrambled for the doorway and nearly collided with the man loitering just outside the den. Strong hands grasped her shoulders, preventing her from walking into a solid wall of muscled chest.

"Thinking about kneeing me again?" he asked, his deep voice a low rumble.

"Thinking about it," she admitted, stepping back until his hands fell away. She didn't want him touching her, and she sure didn't trust herself to touch him.

"I have it coming," he said. "I'm sorry."

For what? Kissing her?

"It doesn't matter," she said, trying to convince them both that she spoke the truth.

"Yes, it does. I realize now that I shouldn't have made any assumptions about you. Eight years ago or now."

"Especially now." She drew in a deep breath. "I don't know what I have to do to convince you that I'm not the screwed-up kid who ran away from here eight years ago." Not kissing him would probably help. But her lips tingled, and she was hungry for another taste of him. This morning he'd reminded her of coffee rather than champagne. She shook her head. "It doesn't matter."

"So were you on the phone with the airline?"

"Sorry to disappoint you, but no. I'm not leaving yet."

Clayton's heart lifted with relief, and he fought the urge to cross the few short steps of hallway separating them and pull her back into his arms. She'd changed out of her running shorts and tank top, but she looked no less sexy in a denim skirt and gauzy pink blouse, the sleeves slipping from her shoulders while the neckline dipped, revealing just a hint of the shadow between her breasts. Clayton's mouth went dry as he looked at her.

"I'm not disappointed that you're staying," he said.

Anger flashed in her eyes. "I wouldn't want you accusing me of leaving you in a mess, if I left now, before Molly comes home."

"I can't blame you for Molly's actions," he said, realizing how unfair he'd been to his sister. He'd acted as if Molly didn't have a mind of her own. "She wouldn't have let you talk her out of something she really wanted to do."

"Not even the tattoo?" she asked, teasing him a little.

"Not even the tattoo," he agreed, shoving his hands into his pockets. He couldn't touch her, because if he did, he might not be able to stop at one kiss.

Abby sighed. "I know when Molly makes up her mind she sticks to her decision. But maybe that's why she's confused. She doesn't really want what she always thought she wanted. Or maybe she realized she wants what she always thought she *didn't* want."

"What are you talking about?"

Abby shrugged. "I don't know. I just... I understand her being confused. But still, it's surprising, her taking off the way she did."

"Through the window." Abby must have had something to do with that. Molly wasn't the type to slip out a window.

"Speaking of taking off, where is everyone? The house is so quiet." She said the last word with such disbelief, as if the house were never quiet.

Clayton remembered only the silence toward the end of his father's life, how he and his mother had worked hard to keep the house quiet so that his father could rest. Then after he died, the house had stayed silent. He glanced toward the doorway behind Abby.

She followed his gaze. "You're not happy that I used Mr. Mick's den."

He shrugged. "It's just that no one uses that room."

Her eyes sparkled with unshed tears. "It must be hard to go in there and not remember."

"I wouldn't know."

She lifted her gaze to his face, her eyes narrowed. "You've not been in there since…"

He shook his head. "No."

"Clayton."

He didn't want to talk about his feelings, because then he might have to actually acknowledge them. "You asked where everyone is. They're in town, getting ice cream."

Her eyes widened in surprise. "Mrs. Mick took Lara without asking me?"

"I told her it would be fine."

Abby didn't take this well. "You're not Lara's parent." No matter what her little girl might wish for. "You have no right to give permission for her to go anywhere. Only I have that right."

"I'm sorry," he said with sincerity.

Somehow she suspected the apology wasn't just for telling his mother to take Lara to town. She thought she understood why he had given his permission as if he had the right. He was used to assuming responsibility for everyone around him. When would he realize she could take care of herself and Lara?

Never. Because he didn't respect her.

"As well as an apology, I guess I owe you a thank-you," he said.

"Clayton McClintock thanking me?" She crossed her arms over her chest and leaned against the wall, careful to not knock off any of the framed photographs of McClintocks that lined the walls as if the hall were an art gallery. She was in a few of the pictures, along with Colleen, Molly, Brenna and Eric.

"Mom says you talked to Rory."

She drew in a breath, clearing her lungs and her mind of the smell of smoke there'd been when she'd caught the boy outside with a cigarette. Despite owing Rory for having snitched all those years ago about the tattoo parlor, she refused to rat him out for his latest transgression. "I hope he listened."

"What did you say to him?" Clayton asked, his jaw tense with stress.

As she'd suspected, Rory had been giving him a hard time. And as she suspected, Clayton would rather have straightened the boy out himself than have had *her* help him.

Among other things, she'd told Rory how damn lucky he was to have people who loved him like his mother and sisters and especially his big brother. Her face flushed as she recalled the things she'd told Rory about his own brother, things he should have known but didn't seem to be aware of. The sacrifices Clayton had made; the responsibilities he'd taken upon himself when his father died to keep the family afloat financially and emotionally.

"Nothing much, really."

Clayton's eyes narrowed, as if he knew she'd omitted something from her answer. "My mom seems to think you've completely turned him around."

She shrugged, causing her blouse to slip farther off one shoulder. Her bra strap slid down along with the gauzy cotton, but she fisted her hand on her hip, refusing to straighten her clothing for Clayton's sake. "I don't know how long my little speech will stick with him." She hoped until he grew up.

"So you have a speech for wayward teens? Do you give it at school assemblies?"

She laughed at his dubious tone. "I just told him how hard I made things for myself when I was a teenager."

"I'd like to hear this speech," he said.

"So you could say I told you so?"

He crossed the short distance between them and swiped his thumb along her cheek. "I worried about you, you know, when you ran away."

Her breath caught in her throat as a result of his gentle touch and his words. "I couldn't stay." Not with her drunken mother. "Eric had left right after..." The funeral. "For the Marines. And in a couple of months Molly and Brenna were leaving for college. There weren't many people left in Cloverville who wanted me here."

"My mom."

She bit her lip and nodded, still sick with regret over the way she'd worried Mrs. Mick. When the older woman had realized she couldn't talk Abby into staying with them, she'd pressed some money on her and a phone card. And she'd sworn that if Abby didn't call her every Sunday she'd send Clayton to bring her home.

"Colleen."

Colleen had probably wanted her to leave

as much as Clayton had. Maybe she shouldn't have made the poor girl keep the secret.

"Not you," she reminded him. "You didn't want me to stay."

"I was…" He expelled a ragged sigh. "Going through a lot back then. I didn't think you'd really leave or that if you did, you'd come back."

Her gaze focused on his lips, she said, "I'm back now."

"But you were gone eight years, living on your own. How did you manage?"

"I didn't turn tricks, if that's what you're asking."

"Abby…"

"Or strip or any other salacious thing you imagined me doing. I worked hard—whatever jobs I could get. Waiting tables, doing dishes, being a short-order cook, babysitting, cleaning hotel rooms. That wasn't the most fun, but for part of my compensation I got a place to stay. I managed."

"You shouldn't have had to 'manage.'" He leaned closer, his mouth almost brushing hers as his fingers slid from her face, down the side of her throat to skim over her bare shoulder. "Alone."

Abby's heart pulsed with desire. She'd

never wanted any other man the way she wanted him. "Clayton…"

"I almost went after you," he admitted, his fingers tracing the ridge of her collarbone. She was so small, so delicate, but for all her curves.

"You did?"

He nodded. "But there was so much going on here. I had to take over the business."

"Had to?"

He had to stop touching her, too, before he lost his mind completely. But her skin was so silky, so warm.

"I always wanted to work in the insurance agency," he said. "But *with* my dad." Not in place of him. Ever since he'd been a kid, he'd planned on working at his father's side.

"Oh, Clayton." She reached up, cupping his face in her palms. "I can't imagine…"

His heart shifted, kicking his ribs as emotions raced though him. He gazed down at her. Her eyes glistened with sympathy and she held on to her bottom lip with her teeth. He reached up, smoothing his thumb over the nibbled flesh. Then he lowered his head to soothe both her lips with his tongue. Something happened to him when he kissed her. All the pain he'd held inside for so long eased.

He *needed* her as he'd never needed anyone.

Clayton's hard body pressed her against the wall and he deepened the kiss. Dizzy with passion, Abby closed her eyes and lowered her arms, gripping his back and clutching his T-shirt in her hands so that she wouldn't fall.

His tongue slid in and out, teasing her with the promise of greater pleasures. Then his mouth moved away from hers, gliding across her cheek. Abby arched her neck and moaned as his lips trailed kisses down her throat.

Goose bumps rose along her skin as her nerves tingled, sensitive to the softest brush of his mouth, the lightest caress of his hands as he skimmed them down her rib cage and over her hips. One hand slid around her back, pressing her closer to where his erection formed a hard ridge beneath the fly of his jeans. Then his other hand traveled back to her shoulder. His fingers stroking her skin, he pushed down the sleeve of her gauzy blouse, shifting the strap of her bra along with the thin cotton. Her breast sprang free of the blouse and the bra, the nipple hard and tilted toward him almost as if begging for his touch.

Abby puffed out a breath through open lips as desire flowed through her body, weakening her muscles so that she melted. "Clayton…"

He didn't make her wait, touching her first with his fingertips, gliding them around the mound before stroking over her nipple.

She arched her back and Clayton's control snapped. How he wanted her. Just a taste.

He lowered his mouth to her breast, pressing kisses along the silky curve. Then he closed his lips around the hard point, sucking it between his teeth, teasing it with his tongue.

Her breath shuddered out while her fingers tunneled into his hair, holding him against her. She moaned.

His hand on her hip traveled lower, moving over her denim skirt until he touched the soft skin of her nicely toned thigh. He brushed the back of her knee, then slid his fingers around to the silky skin on the inside of her thigh. All the while he kept his mouth on her breast, gently tugging at her nipple.

Abby's legs trembled, but she couldn't squeeze them together. Clayton's hand was there, moving under her skirt to the silk of her panties. She opened her mouth to murmur a protest.

But his mouth covered hers, his tongue driving deep between her lips as his fingers stroked beneath the edge of her panties. His other hand cupped her bared breast, stroking over the nipple, which was wet from his tongue. Pleasure streaked through her, burning hotter than anything she'd ever felt before, as his fingers moved inside her.

Her body tightened, then shuddered as an orgasm rippled through her. She sagged against Clayton's hard, hot body, spent. And embarrassed.

"Abby," he murmured, his voice husky as he buried his face in her neck. "Let me take you upstairs. Let me take you…"

Chapter Nine

Abby shook her head. *What had just happened?* How had she lost control like that, with Clayton, who hadn't respected her before and certainly wouldn't now? "I...can't."

Her palms on his chest, she pushed him back. Then, her hands shaking, she pulled up her bra and blouse. But still she felt naked, exposed. She couldn't meet his gaze, she could only feel the heat of it on her.

"I'm sorry," she murmured, hoping he didn't think her a tease, that she'd purposely led him on. But then she remembered Clayton would always think the worst of her. Summoning her pride, she lifted her chin.

Clayton trailed his fingers over her jaw. His voice still thick, he said, "*I'm* sorry."

She met his gaze then, his eyes muddied with all the confusion churning in her stomach. What happened when they were alone together? They *shouldn't* be alone together. She slid along the wall, rattling picture frames as she pulled away from Clayton's loose embrace.

"They went to town?" she asked over her shoulder as she walked, on shaky legs, down the hall toward the kitchen.

Clayton cleared his throat before answering her. "They're walking, and they left just a little while ago."

"I can catch them, then," she said. She wanted to run to town, to run away from the temptation of Clayton's strong arms, of his hot kisses. She couldn't stay alone in an empty house with him, or she'd wind up losing all her self-respect.

"I'll walk with you," he offered.

"Clayton." She suppressed a groan of frustration. Her body still weak from what had just occurred, she needed distance. From him. "I don't need your protection."

He chuckled, the sound of it forced and

rusty. "Hey, I walked here. I have to walk back."

Judging by the muscles in his long legs, she doubted she was the only runner in Cloverville. He probably hadn't walked here, nor had he intended to walk back.

"It'll be dark soon," he said, gesturing toward the kitchen window where the sun shone through the trees surrounding the McClintock house. "So I can use *your* protection."

She fought the smile that twitched her lips. "Cute."

"I'm glad you finally noticed," he said as he stepped closer to her.

She noticed. Even eight years ago, when he'd been so hard on her, she'd noticed. And now—now she couldn't keep her eyes off him. Averting her gaze, she pushed past him and headed toward the door before she changed her mind and took him upstairs with her. They could not remain alone together in an otherwise empty house, or they'd wind up doing something they'd both regret. "Should I lock up?"

"It's Cloverville," he said as an answer.

"So there are no crimes in Cloverville?"

"Not since you left," he quipped.

She swung the door shut, right in his face.

"Hey," he said as he opened it and followed her to the sidewalk. "I was kidding. Lighten up."

She couldn't fight the twitch this time. She smiled and laughed, relieved that he seemed willing to forget what had just happened between them. She could pretend, but she'd never forget. "That's rich coming from you."

"Know what else is rich?" he mused. "You."

Her smile widened with pride and satisfaction. "Not rich. Not yet. But like I've told you, I can take care of myself."

"I checked out your Web site."

"The company Web site," she corrected him.

"Your business seems to be doing well. You have some great testimonials from satisfied clients and employees."

"Your business has been doing well, too," she said, familiar with his accomplishments, since his mother and just about everyone at the reception had sung his praises at length.

His broad shoulders lifted in a shrug. "I just took over the business my father built."

Obviously she could hurt him, too, and her comment about inheriting a business had stung his pride. "You doubled your dad's agency."

"It wasn't hard. Cloverville doubled," he said,

dismissing all his hard work. "And it's great to insure a town that has very little crime, therefore little risk."

"Does that describe your life, too, Clayton? Little risk?"

His gut knotted as if she'd just sucker punched him. Rory's description of his dates and, so, his assessment of Clayton, floated through his mind. Old and boring. At thirty. Abby saw him the same way his fourteen-year-old brother did. Is that why she had refused to come upstairs with him? Despite what had happened in the hall, she doubted he'd really be able to satisfy her?

His body ached, filled with tension and frustration. He could prove her wrong; he could bring her intense pleasure. But she'd been right to turn him down. They had no business being together.

To remind himself, he said, "I have too much responsibility to take stupid risks."

Except for kissing her. He'd taken a risk there, the risk of falling for a woman with whom a relationship could only be messy. For a short while, when he'd lost his head, he'd wanted to take the risk. But there was no place in his plan, in his life, for Abby. And Lara.

"I'm responsible," she said, her voice sharp

with a note of defensiveness. "I worked really hard to make my business what it is today. Before I had Lara, I worked around the clock to succeed."

"I believe you worked hard, but you took a big risk," he argued. "Starting your business, when most start-ups fail, was a huge gamble. And you gamble every time you open another office."

"I'm ready to take another risk," she said.

His heart slammed against his ribs. On him? She wanted to take a risk with him? She'd turned him down in the hall, but she'd been smart to do that. They had no future.

"I want to open an office in Cloverville," she said. "Lease me the space in your building, Clayton."

Abby working beside him day in and day out. And if she worked nights, she'd be working beneath him. Panic pressed down on his chest, stealing his breath. Seeing so much of Abby Hamilton was a risk he couldn't take.

"Hell, no."

Abby had hoped to avoid the man behind the counter, but she should have known there was no avoiding anyone in Cloverville. "Mr.

Carpenter, you're still managing the store all by yourself?"

She was surprised he hadn't sold out or gone under from the pressure of the big-box hardware store built on the outskirts of town. But the people of Cloverville, if nothing else, were loyal.

Even though she'd been gone eight years, loyalty was a permanent part of her makeup, too. If it weren't, she wouldn't still be in town three days after the wedding that wasn't, waiting for Molly to call or come home.

Ah, hell, she wasn't waiting for Molly. She couldn't offer her friend any counsel, not when she was as scared and confused as the runaway bride. She'd dreaded coming back to Cloverville for Molly's wedding, but now she was actually considering opening an office in town. The businesswoman in her validated the location as a sound investment in a growing community. But the disgraced teenager in her just wanted to run again.

Since Clayton wouldn't lease her office space, Mrs. Mick had offered her den as Abby's "home" office. So she'd come to the hardware store for a few things to organize the space: a couple of shelves, some drawer dividers and an in/out box. The items shifted in the precarious pile she'd made on the counter.

"I could use some help," the older man admitted as he rung up the items. "Just during the busy times."

Which she suspected were less and less frequent. She and Lara were the only customers in the store this Tuesday afternoon. The child stood behind Abby, only chancing peeks at the old man behind the counter. Age hadn't mellowed the store owner much. His voice was still a robust bellow.

"I can't keep help," he said, his hearing aid screeching above his raised voice.

Gee, I wonder why...

"Just look at my windows."

She winced, not wanting to be reminded again of her past mistakes. Unlike the colonel, she had actually been responsible for damaging the front of Mr. Carpenter's store. Driving too fast and bad brakes were not a good combination; she'd shared that wisdom as well as a few other bits with Rory when she'd given him the speech the other night. Remembering all the advice she'd given the boy, she lifted her gaze to meet Mr. Carpenter's as she said, "I'm sorry."

He shook his head. "All those streaks on that new glass."

"New glass?"

"Yeah, those Hendrix boys…" He shook his head.

She *had* to meet these Hendrix boys, although she somehow doubted she'd be able to talk sense into them as easily as she had Rory. From what Rory had shared about his friends, they didn't have the loving family he did. They were growing up as Abby had. Unloved. Unwanted. Old bitterness choked her, but she pushed it all down with the bad memories.

"The windows look great," she said.

He shook his head again. "No. I can't reach up like I used to. Damn bursitis." His face flushed as he caught Lara peeking at him, wide-eyed. "Sorry."

"That's okay," she assured the old man. "Staying with the McClintocks, she's already learned some new words."

"That Rory." Mr. Carpenter shook his head. "The boy makes *you* look like an angel." He flushed again as he caught the little girl's rapt gaze. "Uh-huh, your mother was an angel."

Clayton pressed a hand over his face to contain his snort of derision. Abby Hamilton an angel? Not in this lifetime. But he didn't want them to know he'd entered the store. He ducked behind a rack of paint cans, peering through the shelves to where Abby and Lara stood in front of the counter while Mr. Carpenter leaned over the cash register, probably guarding his proceeds from the wild Hamilton girl.

"You are an angel now," Mr. Carpenter said, shocking Clayton as much as he apparently had Abby.

She stepped back, and her blue eyes widened into luminescent circles. "What?"

"Helping people."

"Just Mrs. Hild the other morning…"

"I know about your business, Abby. You done good, girl. You've made Cloverville proud."

Those huge eyes of hers blinked fast and furiously, as if she were fighting the threat of tears. "I didn't know you knew."

"Oh, yes, Mary McClintock brags about you like you're one of her own."

Clayton's mom had spread around town the news of Abby's success? How come he'd never heard about her business until she'd told him the other morning? Oh, yeah, because any time anyone had brought up Abby Hamilton he'd changed the subject, feigning disinterest. He'd obviously been convincing. He'd even convinced himself he'd forgotten about her until she'd walked through the airport terminal, holding the hand of her daughter.

No one could forget about Abby Hamilton. But he had to—the last thing Clayton wanted in his life was more responsibility. He doubted Rory's change of attitude would last, but even if Rory turned into a choir boy Clayton wasn't looking for any more complications in his life.

"You should open up a branch of that business of yours right here in Cloverville," Mr. Carpenter bellowed at her. "I know I could use some temps, someone to help me out when it's busy or to cover for me when I want to go on vacation."

"You take vacations, Mr. Carpenter?" she asked, her voice lilting playfully as she teased the old man.

"The wife's been nagging me to, and maybe she's right. I work too damned hard." He flushed again as he glanced at Lara. "You know about hard work, or you wouldn't have accomplished what you have."

Hard work and focus had been necessary for the success that Abby had achieved. How had she managed it? Maybe he needed to finally accept that she wasn't the girl who'd run away from Cloverville eight years ago. But if he accepted that about her, he might have to accept other things about Abby, like the way she made him feel.

Out of control. Clayton hated being out of control. He still couldn't believe what he'd done to her in the hall outside his father's den, nor could he believe what he'd wanted to do until she'd turned him down and brought him back to his senses.

"Thank you, Mr. Carpenter," she said, her voice breaking with sincerity.

"You should think about it, girl," the old man pressured her.

"I have," she admitted. "I even talked to someone about leasing office space for a branch in Cloverville."

"Where would that be?" the old man asked, lifting a bushy gray eyebrow.

"Right here on Main Street."

"You understand, girl. *This* is Cloverville." He lifted his arms wide, as if encompassing the entire street. "Not those strip malls on the edge of town. We keep up like this, with all those new dang buildings, and we'll be a part of Grand Rapids. We'll lose our identity."

"That'll never happen," Abby assured him.

The old man nodded. "Yeah, we'll always have the colonel."

Abby winced, probably expecting more of the treatment she'd been given eight years ago. The townspeople had been harsh on her, no one more than Clayton had. She'd just been a kid who'd made a stupid mistake. She should have been able to live it down. Clayton moved to the end of the rack, coming around the corner to leap to her defense.

Mr. Carpenter winked at her. "It makes us special. You made us special, honey. You need to come home."

She shook her head. "I was only thinking about opening an office here."

Not about coming home, only opening another branch office. Clayton realized she'd never mentioned moving back to Cloverville, and she'd never admitted to wanting to live here. She'd been bored eight years ago, and that had been before she'd lived in bustling cities. She could never be happy here now.

"You're staying with the McClintocks. So you must know which space is available on Main Street," Mr. Carpenter pointed out.

Abby shrugged. "Yeah, I talked to the landlord," she said, glancing down at her daughter.

He was acting like a fool, Clayton thought,

hiding around the corner to eavesdrop. He stepped out into the aisle behind her and Lara, just as she added, "But the jerk refused to rent to me."

Mr. Carpenter chuckled. "Speak of the devil."

Abby glanced over her shoulder, not even lifting an eyebrow in surprise at his presence. She'd obviously known, the minute he'd entered the store. "Yup," she agreed, "the devil."

"Clayton!" Lara squealed, tugging free of her mother to launch herself into his arms.

Clayton's heart swelled and warmed. "Hey, sweetheart."

Over her little blond head, he met her mother's gaze. Her eyes glittered with concern. Lara had only known him a few days, so how had the little girl gotten so attached to him? Despite having two softhearted sisters, Clayton didn't understand. But he was more concerned about how *he* had gotten so attached to Lara.

Abby rapped her knuckles against the doorjamb before poking her head inside the private office. She drew in a quick breath of surprise at the sight of her most fearless friend with her face buried in her hands. "Hey, Brenna, are you okay?"

The redhead nodded, but wiped her eyes before lifting her gaze to meet Abby's. Red rimmed her green eyes. "I'm fine."

"You've been crying."

Brenna shook her head. "PMS. Don't worry about me."

Usually she wouldn't, but something had been off about Brenna since the minute Abby had returned to town. Or maybe she'd just missed too much over the past eight years by relying on sporadic visits, e-mails and phone calls to keep up with her friends.

Giving Brenna a moment to compose herself, Abby checked out the office. Walls painted to look like Venetian plaster, over-stuffed chairs and antique oak furniture made the space as inviting as a home and reflected the personality of the owner—warm and nurturing.

Concern drew Abby's attention back to Brenna. She was the one who took care of everyone else, like Clayton tried to. So who comforted her?

"You don't cry over PMS," she reminded Brenna.

"Allergies then, making my eyes water."

"Brenna, I hope you know you can talk to me. I won't tell anyone."

The redhead smiled. "I know you'd take my secrets to your grave," she said. "Colleen told me."

"I don't know what you're talking about." It was Colleen's secret to share, not Abby's.

"Have you heard from Molly?" Brenna asked, deftly changing the subject as she wadded up the tissue she'd been clutching and stuffed it in her trash can.

"No. That's why I stopped by." Abby had thought if anyone might have heard from Molly it would have been Brenna, who'd been the maid of honor. But Molly had left *Abby* the note, asking her to stay.

"We could drive over to Eric's."

"And what?" Abby asked. "Break down the door?"

The temper to match her red hair hardened Brenna's deep voice as she admitted, "I wouldn't have a problem with that."

"But they might. And then we what...? Lose *two* friends?"

"So you don't want to do anything? You're content to sit around and wait for her to figure out what she really wants?" Now bitterness was added to Brenna's anger.

She'd obviously had more invested in the wedding than Abby had realized. Or more invested in the groom? Was Brenna developing feelings for her handsome houseguest? Brenna was too loyal to act on an attraction to her friend's man, though. So she wasn't likely to confess her feelings—even to herself.

"I'm never content," Abby reminded her friend. No matter what she accomplished, she felt as if she was missing something; as if she'd failed some test she hadn't even known she'd taken. "I understand Molly being confused. Ever since her dad died, she's thrown herself into school and hasn't taken even a minute to think."

Abby had pretty much done the same thing when she'd left Cloverville. She'd worked hard so that she wouldn't have time to think. But now Molly had brought her back here, forcing her to confront the past that Abby had wanted so badly to leave far, far behind her.

Brenna sighed. "You're right. She deserves to take some time to herself for once."

"Yes." Abby wished she could do the same, not that she wanted time away from her daughter. Just away from Cloverville and Clayton.

"So what are you doing today?" Brenna asked.

"I'm giving Lara a behind-the-scenes look at a bakery."

Brenna stood up and peered around Abby. "Where is she?"

"Your parents stole her from me, the minute I walked through the door."

Brenna laughed. "You may not get her back. They've pretty much stolen Buzz and T.J. from Josh."

"I thought I heard them," Abby said. Even now, back in the wing of offices, peals of laughter could be heard. "Lots of sugar might not be the best idea for them."

"They're good boys." Brenna leapt to the twins' defense. "They've been through a lot."

Abby nodded, unwilling to argue with her friend, whose eyes shone again with tears. "I know." Molly had told her how their mother had taken off when the twins were babies. Until she'd met the handsome Dr. Towers, Abby had figured Molly had accepted his proposal out of pity. She'd always had such a soft a heart. "Josh still staying with your family?"

Her eyes brimming with tears again, Brenna nodded. "He's waiting for Molly to come back."

"*Poor* Molly," Abby said with irony. "Men always fall for her." Since the second grade. Abby had never had that problem. Men never fell for her.

Especially not Clayton. He wouldn't even lease her office space. But, then, he was probably right. She'd be crazy to open a branch of Temps to Go in Cloverville—then she'd *have* to come back here. That was why she hadn't argued with his decision and tried to convince him to change his mind.

"I can't believe how much this place has changed," Abby said, gesturing around the office to draw Brenna back from the depths of her sad mood. "You have a wonderful setup here." While the quaint storefront remained the same on Main Street, the building had been expanded in the back to include a wing of offices and an industrialized kitchen, from which Brenna shipped Kelly Bakery goods to grocery stores throughout the Midwest.

Brenna settled an ample hip on the corner of her desk. A smile of pride brightened her round face. "See, you can run a successful business from Cloverville."

"Et tu, Brenna?"

The redhead laughed. "Yes, I think you should open an office in Cloverville. I think you should stay here, and not just until Molly comes back. You should stay here for *good*. It's home."

Abby sighed. "No, Brenna, it's not."

Brenna reached out, closing her hands around Abby's shoulders. Her green eyes glinted with knowledge. She'd seen the kiss on the dance floor. Abby just knew it.

Abby braced herself, waiting for the taunts she'd earned by kissing their childhood enemy.

But what Brenna said was worse than any taunt. "Home is where the heart is, honey."

Abby clasped her hand around the sponge, squeezing sudsy water between her fingers. Then she pushed the foam square against the window of Carpenter's Hardware. Washing Mr. Carpenter's windows wasn't as strenuous as the run she'd just finished, but she needed to expend some more of her nervous energy. Or she'd never get to sleep tonight and she'd already lain awake too many nights, staring at the ceiling in Clayton's old room. Violating his privacy, Abby had snuck into Clayton's room on more than one occasion when they'd been growing up. Unlike his brother Rory, Clayton had never indulged in posters of sports figures or scantily clad supermodels. The walls had been stark white, the floor cold, bare wood.

After he'd moved out, his mother had redone the room so it resembled an upscale hotel room, and Abby had no reason for not being able to sleep. Except that she lay there, imagining how much more pleasure Clayton could have given her if she'd come upstairs with him, if she'd lain with him in his old bedroom.

"First Mrs. Hild's flowers, now Mr. Carpenter's windows," intoned a deep male voice. "Are you doing penance for your past sins?"

He was the reason she couldn't sleep. Her hand tightened around the sponge and water squirted out, hitting her face and the front of her tank top. The dousing did nothing to cool her temper.

"I have to help Mrs. Hild and Mr. Carpenter myself, because you won't rent me a space so that I can open an office here and provide temps for people who need them."

"You can open your franchise someplace else," he said, dismissing her. Dismissing the need for her business in Cloverville.

Although she'd accepted long ago that he didn't respect her, the realization still stung. She shouldn't care what Clayton McClintock thought of her. She shouldn't care about him, at all. She couldn't fool herself into actually believing that, but maybe she could fool *him*.

"Don't trust yourself in the same town with Abby Hamilton?" she teased as she turned toward him.

Hell, no. He gritted his teeth to hold in the groan that was building in the back of his throat. Water streaked down her throat, over the curve of breast exposed by the low neckline of her damp tank top. Some country singer once had sung about a woman wearing a white tank top, but until now he'd never understood the fascination.

"Don't trust Abby Hamilton," he said. But she was right. He didn't trust himself around her. He bunched his hands and shoved them into his pockets, so he wouldn't reach for her as he had in the hall the other night; so he wouldn't lose control and want more from her than he could handle.

He cleared his throat, thick with desire for her. "I'm not stopping you from opening an office in Cloverville. There're other spaces available for lease."

"Come on, Clayton. You heard Mr. Carpenter," she said, calling him on his eavesdropping. "Your space is perfect. If I go into one of those strip malls, he'll consider it a betrayal of Cloverville."

"If he can forgive you for mutilating the

town founder, I think he'll be able to forgive you for not opening your business on Main Street."

"He can forgive me," she agreed. "So can Mrs. Hild. Why can't you, Clayton?"

Because he wouldn't let himself. He needed some excuse to help him fight his crazy attraction to her. But he had other reasons to avoid getting in deeper with Abby. Although as she stretched and reached, pushing her breasts against the damp cotton of her ribbed shirt, he couldn't think of any of those reasons. In fact, he couldn't think at all.

She leaned over the bucket of water and squeezed out the sponge, then reached up and continued washing windows. "Why can't you forgive me?" she asked him again, almost offhandedly, as if she didn't really care that he hadn't. "Why can't you see what everyone else has—that I've changed?"

God, he knew she'd changed. She was a successful businesswoman, a loving mother. She was an exceptional woman who deserved someone with more than he had left to offer.

"We both know I see you differently now," he pointed out, knowing that she probably couldn't forget their kisses, either. But did she lay awake, just as he did, wanting more? Wanting him as hungrily as he wanted her?

"What do you see, Clayton?" she asked as she worked on rinsing the windows. In the reflection of the clean glass sparkling in the sun, she held his gaze. "What do you see when you look at me?"

"Trouble." For his peace of mind. For his heart.

"Then you don't see me any differently." She sighed and tossed the sponge down on the sidewalk before reaching for the bucket. "And since you still see me as a troublemaker, I might as well make some trouble."

Clayton's breath caught in his chest as Abby stepped closer, her body nearly touching his. Then she tipped the bucket of water over his head. Soap bubbles clung to his lashes, some popping, some escaping to float away.

The plastic bucket clattered against the cement when it dropped to the sidewalk and then bounced off the sponge and rolled to a stop against the dark brick at the front of the hardware store.

Abby's hand shot to her mouth, holding in a gasp of surprise, but Clayton just stood there, water and suds dripping from his hair and chin. Wet, his black knit polo shirt molded to every impressive muscle on his chest, and his khakis clung to his lean hips and long legs.

With her attention on his long, narrow feet, she didn't notice that he'd moved until his arms were around her, spinning her so that her back pressed against the damp glass of the windows she'd just washed.

"You want to play?" He uttered the words as a threat, his voice a deep rumble in the chest that was pressed tight against hers.

Chapter Ten

She mocked him gently. "You don't know how to play, Clayton."

Realization that she was right staggered him. He *didn't* know how to play. In thirty years, Clayton had never learned to have fun.

Abby lifted her arms, wrapping them around his neck as she rose up on tiptoe. When she pressed her lips to his, he stood as still as he had when she'd dumped the bucket over his head; as shocked by her kiss as he'd been by his dousing.

She pulled back. "See, you should lease me that space," she told him. "You need me."

"Abby…" His eyes darkened as he stared down at her.

She knew better than to hold her breath waiting for him to agree with her. But she didn't expect the burst of warm water. She sucked in a breath, then screamed, "Clayton!"

He dropped the wrung-out sponge back on the sidewalk. He'd moved fast when he grabbed her, and she hadn't even seen him pick up the sodden block of foam. As he looked at her now, his chest shook with laughter.

Abby sucked in another breath. She couldn't get over the transformation of Clayton's face when he laughed. With his dark hair and eyes and chiseled features, he was always handsome. But at this moment he was also happy—his eyes warmed and they sparkled, and his cheeks creased with a grin.

She'd been teasing him a moment ago about needing her. Now, however, she wondered who needed whom.

She knotted her fingers in the wet fabric of his shirt and pulled herself up so that her lips, still tingling from the previous contact with his, could brush over his mouth again. Once. Twice.

He groaned, then stroked his fingertips through her curls, holding her head steady while he deepened the kiss. Her pulse racing, Abby opened her lips for the bold exploration of his tongue. She lost herself in his kiss. In Clayton.

Until the bell jangled above the hardware door, as a customer entered the store. Clayton jerked back, leaving her arms to drop to her sides. Had he realized, as she had only now, that they were making out on Main Street? Cloverville's busybodies would have a field day with this one. And if his mother heard about it, she'd be relentless in her matchmaking.

Abby chanced a glance at Clayton's face, but he wasn't looking at her, or even looking around to see who'd witnessed their kissing.

"Damn, I'm going to be late," he said, his attention on his watch.

"What? Missing a hot date?" Abby fought back the jealousy—she had no reason for it. Clayton meant nothing to her. And she meant less than nothing to him, despite what they'd nearly done a few nights before. He was probably glad she'd turned him down.

"No hot date, but I have someplace I have to be." He glanced around then, as if he'd just noticed where they were. "Where's Lara?"

"With your mom." The two of them had become so attached that Abby worried about how she'd separate them when she and Lara left Cloverville.

"I should thank her."

"Your mom?"

"Lara." His voice and eyes softened when he said the child's name.

Her breath caught. She already worried that Lara was becoming too fond of him. Was he beginning to fall for the little girl? She hoped not; she and Clayton could never have a future. Only these few stolen kisses.

"Why do you want to thank my daughter?"

"For taking off some of the must-have-grandchildren-now pressure that Mom's been putting on me."

Abby actually thought Lara had made the situation worse with Clayton's mother, as she was probably the main reason for Mrs. Mick's attempts at matchmaking.

"Well, you're thirty years old and not even dating anyone," she pointed out. "She has reason to worry about you."

"I *was* dating someone," he said, his admission causing jealousy to course through her again.

She had no right to such an emotion, no claim at all on Clayton. "That's right." The woman who'd dumped him. "Erin."

"Ellen."

"So why did she break up with you?" Why would any woman break up with a man as successful, responsible and passionate as Clayton McClintock?

"I was going to be late to pick her up for a date."

"She sounds like she's high-maintenance."

"No, she wasn't. She was just sick of coming last, after everything else in my life." A weary sigh slipped through his lips.

As Abby had suspected, Clayton had taken too much on himself after his father died. Once she thought he'd have enjoyed being in charge, but now she realized he harbored some resentment over all the responsibility.

"I avoid high-maintenance," he said as his smoldering gaze skimmed her wet hair and clothes.

"*I'm* not high-maintenance," she said with a laugh. She'd never had anyone but herself to maintain her, so she'd learned to never expect much from anyone *but* herself.

"I know, Abby, but I still want to avoid you."

His admission hit her like a sharp slap. She drew her head back. "I could always count on you to be honest with me."

"I am being honest with you. I want to avoid anything serious, Abby."

"This," she said, gesturing toward her wet hair and clothes, "isn't serious. We're just goofing around."

"Goofing around?" he repeated the phrase as if he'd never heard it before.

"I'm not even staying in Cloverville." But the truth was, she'd begun to consider opening more than an office. She'd thought about opening up her heart—to Clayton. Good thing his honesty had saved her from making another mistake.

"So you really don't want the empty office?" he asked. With a trace of disappointment?

"I still want the office. I think Cloverville would be an ideal location for my third branch of Temps to Go."

"But Cloverville wouldn't be an ideal location for Abby Hamilton?"

"It never was," she reminded him. "So don't worry. I'm not looking for a husband. Or even a boyfriend." She'd learned long ago that she couldn't trust anyone to love her. "I just want an office space."

"I never would have thought you and I would have something in common."

"An aversion to relationships." She'd acquired hers by way of necessity and self-preservation. How had Clayton, with the positive example of his parents' loving marriage, come by his?

"I have two plans," he told her. "One's for the business. I want to expand the agency and my investments even more, make sure there's enough money for Mom to live comfortably and to put Rory through college. Of course, he has to make it through high school first."

"He will," she assured his concerned big brother. She'd nag Rory until he did. "So is your other plan personal?" If so, that was the plan that interested her far more.

He nodded. "That plan's a lot shorter."

"No lofty goals?"

"Just one. To stay single." The insurance agent in him explained, "I'm not willing to take a risk like marriage or children."

Her breath hitched with the awareness of why he considered her high-maintenance. Because she was a single mother, Clayton had probably automatically assumed she was on the prowl for a daddy for her daughter.

"You sound determined," she observed.

"I am. I've taken on all the responsibility I can handle."

"Then I guess your mother will just have

to accept the fact you're never going to give her grandchildren."

"Yes, she will." He glanced at his watch again. "I'm really late. I have to go."

Standing in a puddle of soapy water, Abby watched Clayton walk away. Mrs. Mick wasn't the only one who'd have to accept that Clayton was never going to settle down. He wanted no wife, no children, no more responsibilities.

Abby blinked against the water dripping from her hair into her eyes. The soap stung them and made them tear.

"How'd you get all wet?" Colleen asked her as Abby stormed into the McClintocks' sun-filled kitchen. "There's not a cloud in the sky."

"Oh, there is," Abby assured her. "There's been a dark cloud hanging over my head since the minute I came back to Cloverville."

A laugh sputtered out of Colleen as she rose from the stool she'd been sitting on. "How very Eeyore of you. You've been watching too many *Winnie the Pooh* videos with Lara."

"You know that black cloud," Abby insisted as she walked over to the refrigerator and opened the freezer compartment. She reached for a sugar-free Popsicle. "You call it Clayton."

Colleen laughed again. "Clayton, a black cloud? The description fits him pretty well." And she didn't know half of what had happened between Abby and Clayton.

Abby inwardly sighed. Clayton had been honest with her. She wasn't mad at him; she was mad at herself, for being disappointed.

When was she going to learn to have no expectations? Lara's father should have taught her the lesson, once and for all, that just because a man *seemed* responsible, it didn't mean he was.

"Where've you been?" she asked the younger woman. "I've hardly seen you at all the past few days. And you live here."

Colleen blushed from the point of her widow's peak to the tip of her pinky toes. "I—I…"

Curiosity drew Abby's attention away from her frozen treat. "Colleen, what have you been up to?"

"N-n-nothing."

"You've talked to Molly!" Abby pointed a grape Popsicle at her. "She's fine and there's no reason for me to stay here any longer. You're all just conspiring to keep me here."

But Clayton. Clayton wanted her gone, so he could avoid her. So he could avoid any serious involvement. Didn't he realize that his family wasn't enough, that he needed more in his life?

He needed her.

Abby shook her head. No, no one but Lara had ever needed her.

"I swear I haven't talked to Molly," Colleen insisted, the color in her face fading to paleness. "I wish I could, though."

Abby narrowed her eyes, trying to gauge the younger woman's mood. "Are *you* okay?"

"Of course. I'm fine," Colleen assured her, even as her voice trembled with emotion. "I understand Molly being confused and needing time to think."

Abby sighed. "Yeah, so do I."

"Too bad other people wouldn't honor her request," Colleen grumbled.

"Clayton giving you a hard time, too?"

"Hmm… Clayton?"

"He suspects I know where Molly is." Not that he'd bugged her a whole lot about Molly. They'd talked about other things, or they hadn't talked at all. Abby shivered.

"You should get out of those clothes. How'd you get so wet, really?" Colleen asked.

"I was washing Mr. Carpenter's windows." When Clayton had interrupted her, just like he had her sleep every night since she'd returned.

"Okay." With that single word her friend accepted her explanation, while simultaneously letting Abby know she was aware that a lot more than window-washing had taken place.

"Mrs. Mick still out with Lara?" she asked, then bit on the Popsicle to finish it.

"I don't know where they are," Colleen said. "I just got home."

Since it was already well after closing time at the insurance agency, Abby wanted to ask where she'd been, but she withheld the question. Since Colleen had accepted her explanation, Abby had to reciprocate. "Mrs. Mick took Lara to Rory's soccer game today."

Colleen nodded. "Clayton left work early to go to the game."

But he hadn't gone straight to the soccer field. He would have had to change his clothes first. "So he made you close up the office, instead of going to the game?"

"He has to be there. He's the coach."

He coached the games. No wonder Mrs. Mick wasn't back yet with Lara—no doubt, the game had started late. And maybe Clayton had suggested ice cream again. Abby's heart clenched. She worried about her daughter's growing attachment to Cloverville and especially to certain residents of the town.

"I don't know who Lara has the bigger crush on," Abby said. "Rory...or Clayton?"

Colleen shook her head. "I can't imagine anyone having a crush on either of them. But at least Rory can sometimes be fun."

"Does Clayton ever lighten up?" Abby asked. When he wasn't with her, that is?

Her young friend shrugged. "Actually, he can be a lot of fun, too, when he lets himself relax."

"How often does that happen?"

"Not often."

Abby shouldn't care. They weren't friends. They really weren't *anything*. But her heart shifted in her chest, aching for him. He'd had to grow up much too fast, but then again so had she. They had a lot in common.

Colleen slid her arm around Abby's shoulders. "Don't let him get to you. If you'd let me tell him the truth..."

"No!" Abby's voice cracked as she shouted out the word.

"But that's why he has such a problem with you," Colleen said, her voice thick with regret. "He thinks you hurt me, when it was actually…"

"The past, Colleen. It doesn't matter. The town's forgotten about it. Even Mrs. Hild and Mr. Carpenter have forgotten about it." Or if not forgotten, at least forgiven.

"Turning the reception into a welcome-back party for you and Lara was brilliant."

"Your mother *is* brilliant." Sometimes she wondered if the McClintock children realized just how lucky they were to have her.

"The way everyone responded had to prove to you that the town does really welcome you back." Colleen squeezed her shoulders. "You can move home now, Abby."

The remains of the Popsicle melting in her hands, Abby pulled away from Colleen to walk over to the sink. "Cloverville is *not* home."

"So where is home? I know you've packed up the apartment in Chicago."

"I had a reservation in Raleigh." Which she'd had to cancel, since Molly still hadn't come home or phoned her. "When I lost Miss Ramsey, it was time to move out of the city."

"It's time to move back home."

"Colleen…"

"I want you to move back here," she said

as she joined Abby by the sink. "Then maybe I won't feel so guilty."

Abby washed off her fingers, then dried her hands and gave her slim friend a hug. "Don't. I don't regret anything, and neither should you."

"But I do," Colleen said, her pretty eyes glistening with unshed tears. "Please think about moving back. I'm sure Lara would love growing up in Cloverville."

Abby was also pretty sure her daughter would love growing up where Abby had always wanted to grow up, in the McClintock house.

But that wasn't possible. For either of them.

"Can we go to the school, Mommy?" Lara asked, tipping her head back to stare up with a beseeching gaze.

Abby smiled. Despite the two years of preschool she'd had, Lara still couldn't wait to start "real" school. She'd be in kindergarten in the fall, and she'd made Abby promise to find a school district where she'd have to ride a big yellow bus.

"Honey, school is out for the summer." Abby's arms strained as she pushed her daughter higher on the swings at Cloverville Park.

"But the school swings are bigger. I saw them last night when we were there for Rory's game. When the game was done, Clayton pushed me on them." Her voice rose with awe. "He pushed me *really* high."

Good for Clayton. Resentment burned in Abby's heart. He was so good with her daughter. If he had no intention of getting "involved," he shouldn't be so sweet to the child. She sighed, suspecting he couldn't help himself. Clayton had always been a natural father figure. He should have some kids of his own. But, then, they weren't part of his "plan."

Abby could understand that. And falling in love, giving her heart to someone who didn't want any part of it, wasn't in *her* plan, either.

"Why can't you push me high like Clayton?" Lara asked, looking back at her mother over her shoulder.

"He has longer arms and legs than I do," Abby explained.

"He's really big," Lara agreed, sounding awestruck.

"Yeah, really big." Abby's face flushed as her thoughts detoured to parts of Clayton other than his arms and legs. She wondered…

"Speak of the devil," Lara said.

"What?" Abby asked, waving a hand in front of her sweaty face.

"Isn't that what you say when Clayton walks up and you're talking about him?"

"Yes, she calls me the devil," Clayton agreed as he joined them near the swing set. He wore a white T-shirt and navy-blue running shorts above his long legs.

He was a handsome devil. His brown hair, disheveled by the brisk morning breeze, tempted her fingers.

"I'm not wrong," Abby murmured, just for his ears, as she leaned closer to him. "You are the devil."

Her breath caressed his throat, raising the short hairs on the nape of his neck. He stepped closer, until his shoulder brushed against hers. Then he put his hand over hers on the seat of Lara's swing, giving the little girl such a big push that she squealed with delight.

"Higher! Higher!" she shouted, her face flushed with excitement and her eyes warm with affection as she looked down at Clayton.

Clayton's heart shifted in his chest. Damn, she was getting to him. And so was her mother. "You girls are up early."

"So are you," Abby pointed out.

"I was out for a run." He couldn't sleep much, not with thinking about Abby.

"Do you have ADD, too?" Lara asked.

"What? No, I don't have it." Clayton was mesmerized by Lara, who tipped her head back to smile at him, her curls nearly brushing the wood chips on the ground beneath the swing set. "Do you?"

"No," Abby answered for her daughter. "*I* have it."

Clayton blew out a short breath. "Well, that explains a few things."

"Explains, not excuses," she said, realizing that his knowing about her ADD made no difference to Clayton.

"Don't put words in my mouth," Clayton protested.

Lara's eyes widened with interest in this adult conversation.

"You can pump your legs and swing by yourself for a minute," Abby told her daughter now as she wrapped her fingers around Clayton's forearm and pulled him away from the swing set. Muscles tightened and warmed beneath her grasp. Fingers tingling, she released him and stepped back. "I can put words in your mouth because I know what you think, Clayton—at least about me."

"And I know what you think about me." He chuckled. "I'm not the devil, Abby."

"Neither am I, and I'm sick of you treating me like one." She shifted deeper into the odd shadow cast by the park's statue of Colonel Clover, tempted to tell Clayton the truth about the night the statue took its disastrous battering. But the secret was not hers to tell, and knowing the truth wouldn't make any difference to Clayton.

"Abby…"

"There's nothing I can do to convince you to let me lease the office space from you?"

He shook his head. "It took you eight years to come back. You hate this town. Why would you want to open an office here now, when you said yourself that you have no intention of moving back?"

"You really don't want me to have any reason to even *visit* Cloverville," she said, fully understanding why he kept refusing to lease her the space.

"I don't care if you visit," he insisted. "I don't care what you do."

"Liar," she accused him, realizing that for the first time in their lives, Clayton hadn't been honest with her. But she suspected he wasn't being honest with himself, either. "If you didn't care, you'd lease me the space."

"You don't need that office. There're other available spaces to lease."

"So you don't care if I open an office in Cloverville," she concluded. "You just don't want it to be next to yours. You don't want me that close to you?"

He had been honest when he'd admitted to wanting to avoid her. But, then, why did he keep kissing her?

"I'm afraid if I have much more contact with you, I'm going to wind up like the colonel," he admitted, gesturing toward the statue. "Broken to pieces after you run me over on your way out of town."

"Clayton…"

"C'mon, Abby," he said, "the ADD explains a lot, and it makes you an even bigger risk for me. You're going to get bored and change your mind. Maybe you'll break the lease."

But he worried about her breaking something besides the lease, as well. He worried about his heart. She was the only one who'd ever come close to derailing his plan not to fall in love. Abby and Lara. They touched something inside him that he'd closed off for so long. He couldn't risk opening his heart. He couldn't risk the kind of pain that his mother had barely survived when she'd lost his father.

And he *would* lose Abby. She wouldn't stay in Cloverville. Neither the town nor he could hold her interest for long.

He glanced toward the old statue of the colonel. The neck weld had broken again, and the head, with its dented helmet and mangled ear, lay in the bushes beneath the colonel's feet.

He could identify. Every time he was around Abby Hamilton, he lost his head. But he couldn't lose his heart over her, too.

"I wouldn't break the lease. I've been running my business for a while, Clayton," she reminded him. "I *stuck* with it."

He lifted a brow, skeptical. "But to launch a business, to sign clients, you'd have to spend a lot of time here. You'd have to move back to Cloverville, at least for a while." Would she consider it?

"I have an office in Detroit, and I haven't lived there for a few years," she answered.

"But you lived there when you started the business," he argued. "Just like you did in Chicago."

Abby's eyes stung with unshed tears. It wasn't that Clayton didn't trust her or respect her that kept him from leasing the office space. He just didn't want her around him. At all. "We both know you don't want me staying in Cloverville, anyway. That's why you won't lease me the space."

"I'm not going to tie myself up in a lease that you'll only wind up breaking," he explained. "You're used to living in the big city. This town is too boring for you—you'd lose interest fast."

Were they really talking about Cloverville? Or did *he* want her interest and worry that he couldn't keep it, that he couldn't keep her? "Clayton…"

"And when you take off this time, you're going to break someone's heart," he said.

Abby's breath caught and burned in her lungs as she stared up at Clayton's face, trying to read his feelings. But he wasn't looking at her. He'd turned back toward the swing set.

And Lara.

Lara, whose heart was bound to break if she got any more attached to Cloverville and the McClintocks.

"You're right," Abby agreed.

She knew what she had to do.

Chapter Eleven

"What are you doing?"

Abby glanced up in response to her friend's question. Colleen stood in the doorway, her eyes dark with concern. Abby returned her attention to her packing, her hands shaking as she folded clothes into an open suitcase. If only Mrs. Mick didn't keep unpacking it… "I think it's obvious."

"But why are you leaving now?" Colleen asked. "I thought you were actually considering moving here."

"Opening an office, yes. Moving here?" She couldn't lie. "I considered it."

"I wish you'd open an office in Cloverville," Colleen enthused. "I could help you run it."

"Sure, Clayton would love that," she remarked with a derisive snort. "My stealing away his office manager—"

"If he rented you the space next door, I could manage both, with a little help. Mom even said she'd like to work for you."

Abby had wanted Mrs. Mick to become Lara's new caregiver. The older woman made no secret of her feelings for the little girl— she already loved her. "Well, Clayton won't lease to me, so it doesn't matter."

"He's an idiot," his sister said. "You can lease a space somewhere else in Cloverville, and I'll just quit him and come to work for you."

Abby laughed. "That'll make him love me."

And wasn't that the problem? Panic pressed tight against her heart. She *wanted* Clayton to love her. Why? Had she gone and fallen for him even though she knew they could have no future? Clayton could never love her, and Abby refused to settle for anything less than love. She and Lara deserved more.

She snorted in disgust at her own thoughts. "Like that would ever happen."

Colleen's brown eyes brightened. "It won't if you take off."

"I don't want Clayton to..." She couldn't even say it aloud. She couldn't think it.

"Abby, you're falling for Clayton," her friend proclaimed, clasping Abby's wrist so that she had to stop packing. "That's wonderful."

"It's impossible. We hate each other."

"You know what they say about the fine line between love and hate," Colleen teased. "Can you tell me that you really hate him?"

Abby bit the inside of her cheek, but she was numb to the pain. "No. But I wish I did." Then she wouldn't care that he'd never love her.

"I understand," the younger woman said.

Abby realized that Colleen hadn't been around the house for a reason. She'd been busy falling for someone, too—someone who couldn't or wouldn't love her back.

"I have to leave, Colleen." Before she fell so hard that she tossed aside all her self-respect.

"You're going to break Lara's heart."

Not Clayton's—his sister didn't presume to claim he loved Abby. She'd never been more grateful for her friendship with this McClintock. She and Colleen respected each other too much to lie *to* each other, just *for* each other.

Abby nodded. "That's why we have to leave now, before she gets any more attached."

"What if it's already too late?" Colleen asked.

That fear had Abby's stomach tied into tight little knots. What if it was already too late for both Lara and *her?*

"We've moved a lot over the years," she reminded Colleen. "Moving to different areas of Detroit and Chicago, different apartments. Lara's pretty resilient."

And so was she. She'd handle leaving Cloverville a second time. Hell, it wasn't as if she'd ever really been back—she'd only been visiting.

Colleen released her wrist, but said, "I thought you were going to wait until we heard from Molly."

Abby felt a twinge of guilt. "I can't stay…"

"Not even for Molly?" Colleen persisted. She'd make a great mother someday, Abby thought, since she expertly wielded guilt as a weapon. But, then, she understood guilt fairly well.

Poor Colleen. Abby hated leaving her as much as she hated leaving Mrs. Mick and Rory and…

But she had to leave.

"Molly's smart." The smartest one of all of

them. She'd been class valedictorian in high school, on the dean's list in college, and she probably would have graduated with honors from medical school if she hadn't taken time off to plan her wedding. "She'll figure out what she wants."

And unlike Abby, she would be able to *get* what she wanted.

"What about you?" Colleen asked. "Are you fine?"

"I will be, once I get out of here." God, she hated lying to her friends and herself.

Clayton, nerves shot from his most recent early-morning run-in with Abby, jumped when his office door slammed. He sloshed coffee over the rim of his mug, leaving wet brown circles on the files on his desk. Maybe he'd have to give up drinking coffee.

"Clayton!" His youngest sister stood over his desk, her face bright with exasperation. "Why are you being such an ass?"

His head snapped back, as if she'd slapped him. Colleen had never spoken to him in such a manner before. Of all his siblings, he'd always gotten along with Colleen best. Which was why she'd come to work for him. And he didn't know what he'd do without her. "Colleen, I don't know what it is that you think I've done."

He'd already been planning on giving her a raise; the business was doing great despite competition from some new insurance offices in the strip malls on the outskirts of Cloverville. Thanks to his father, Cloverville residents trusted the McClintock name.

"You're running Abby out of town."

"I haven't done anything to Abby." Other than kiss her. He could still feel the softness of her lips against his, and he could taste the sweetness that was hers alone. How he wished he'd done more than kiss her.

No, he would have been a great deal smarter to never kiss her at all. Abby Hamilton had never been anything but trouble. He clung to that belief even though he knew how untrue it was. Abby was a smart businesswoman and a wonderful mother. Even so, she would always be trouble to Clayton.

"You won't lease her the office."

"She can lease another office, if she really wants to open a business in Cloverville," he pointed out, tired of having to take the heat over his decision. Even Mr. Carpenter was giving him trouble, claiming to be out of lightbulbs the other day, despite boxes of bulbs Clayton had glimpsed in the back.

"She wants *this* space."

Why? Why did she want to be so close to him, when she knew how he felt about marriage and children? He'd been honest with her, and he wished she would be honest with him. But, then, maybe she hadn't been honest with herself, if she really thought their kisses had been nothing more than goofing around.

"I don't trust Abby Hamilton," he said. Actually, he didn't trust himself around her.

"She's leaving, Clayton. She's packing right now."

He sucked in a breath, almost as if Colleen had shoved his desk into his stomach. His hand shook as he reached for his coffee mug, pushing it toward the corner of his blotter and out of his reach. "I thought she was going to stick around until she heard from Molly. Has she called yet?"

Colleen shook her head. "No, she hasn't."

"Some loyal friend, huh? Taking off before she hears that Molly's all right," he huffed, shaking his head as if disgusted. He was, but only with himself. He should be happy—or at least relieved—that she was leaving. But all he felt was regret and a sense of the loss he'd wanted to avoid.

"This isn't about Molly. It's about *you*." His sister confirmed his suspicions.

He'd run Abby out of town a second time, with his cold disapproval. Except that he didn't disapprove of her. He was damn proud of her. All the time he'd spent worrying about her over the past eight years had been for nothing.

"Why won't you give Abby a break?"

"I can't." Because she might break *him,* or at least his heart.

"Is this still about Colonel Clover?" his kid sister demanded to know.

Clayton should let her believe that it was. He didn't want to admit to his real reason for keeping Abby at arm's length. His feelings. How easily he could fall for her, if he let himself.

He sighed and pushed a hand through his hair. "Damn it, Colleen. You've worked here for a couple of years now. You understand that the insurance business is all about risk. I can't take a risk on Abby Hamilton."

"She didn't run into the colonel."

"What?" It had all happened so long ago that he really didn't care. Abby wasn't the wild young teen she'd once been. He knew that.

"*I* did, Clayton."

"You don't have to lie for her. I really don't..."

"She's the one who lied," Colleen said. "For me. She knew what our family was going through with Daddy dying, and she didn't want me to get in trouble for driving without a license, for stealing her car..."

"Colleen, you wouldn't have done any of that," he said. Because then he'd failed *her,* too, as well as his dad. When his father had been diagnosed with terminal cancer, Clayton had promised to take care of his siblings. Protect them. He hadn't done a very good job. Rory was out of control, and the promises he'd made were probably only manipulation to get him out of trouble. Molly had run out on her wedding, humiliating a good man and disappointing two young boys. And now Colleen was lying.

"I stole Abby's car, Clayton. I was going to run away because..."

Because of their father dying. Because of how unhappy their family had been. Because they hadn't been able to help the man they'd loved the most. He stood up and walked around his desk to pull her into his arms. "I know."

He'd been tempted to run away, too.

"Then I crashed the car. I don't know how

Abby ever managed to drive that piece of junk. The steering and brakes were crap. And *I* hit the colonel."

She trembled in his arms, as if reliving the experience. She'd been so banged up, badly scratched and bruised. He should have known then that she had to have been behind the wheel. But it had been easier to assume the worst of Abby, who'd screwed up before, than of his sister. "Abby wasn't even in the car," he said, realizing now why she hadn't had a scratch on her.

"She found me in the park," Colleen explained. "She pushed me out of the driver's seat and took the blame, and she did it to protect me. She wouldn't let me tell the truth."

"But she got expelled." Not to mention all the abuse she'd taken from him. The names he'd called her ricocheted in his head, taunting him. He'd been the idiot, not her. Then and now.

"That's the kind of person Abby Hamilton is," Colleen said, her voice shaking with emotion as tears streamed down her face. "She's the most loyal and loving friend a person can have. She wouldn't let me tell. Ever."

She sniffled. "She won't be happy that I've told you now, either. But I think you need to understand what kind of person Abby really is."

"I know."

"She's worth taking a risk on, Clayton."

Apparently Colleen had learned the insurance business better than he had. Some risks were worth the possibility of loss. But could he do it? Could he open up the heart he'd closed off so many years ago?

"If you want to keep her here, I think it's going to take more than a lease. You've really given her a hard time," his wise little sister pointed out.

"I don't think Abby wants anything from me *but* a lease." Not after what he'd put her through. He didn't deserve another chance, when he'd refused again and again to give her one.

"It might be too late, Clayton," Colleen warned him. "Abby was almost done packing when I left her."

"Then maybe I should just let her leave." That would be the smart thing to do. The safe thing. But his sister was right. It was time for Clayton to take a risk.

Indignation coursed through Abby, so that her hands shook when she shoved open the door to Clayton's office. But was she mad at *him* or at *herself?* Just because he'd called and told her to come down to the office didn't mean she had to come. Or even that she *should.*

She should be on a flight to… Anywhere out of Cloverville, Michigan. Away from Clayton McClintock. And instead, she'd come to see him.

Just one last time. Then she would call the airport as soon as she got back to the house. Or maybe she'd use Clayton's phone at the agency to reserve a flight. He'd probably be only too happy to dial the airline number for her.

"Clayton?" she called out as she entered the deserted reception area of his office. The insurance agency had closed more than an hour earlier, according to the sign on the door—the one he'd left unlocked for her. She reached toward the counter, running her finger around the rim of a crystal candy dish. Clayton had replaced the old desktop computers with flat screens and updated the older, multiline phones to modern headset models. He'd also made use of fresh paint and new carpet, but the presence of this simple candy dish told Abby that he'd kept his father's spirit there as part of the agency. The generous heart of it.

"In here." The deep voice emanated, not from a doorway into what she assumed was his private office, but from out in the hall somewhere.

She turned back toward the foyer, crossing a small vestibule containing an old-fashioned gum-ball machine to reach the other half of the main floor and the empty office space. The door stood open now, although she was sure it had been closed when she'd passed by a moment earlier.

"Hello?" she called out as she walked into the reception area. Not a desk or even a cardboard box sat atop the gray Berber carpeting.

"Back here."

Her frustration growing, she followed the low rumble of his voice through to a private office in the back. "Clayton, you're not my big brother. You can't order me around like you do the rest of your family."

"I'm glad I'm not your brother," he said as he rose from a table set in the middle of the empty office. A crisp linen tablecloth fell, in graceful folds, to the carpet. Between a pair of sparkling crystal wineglasses, two tapered candles flickered, their flames reflected in the silver covers topping two serving platters.

Mesmerized—and mystified—she asked, "What is all of this?"

"An apology." As she looked back, again, to the table, to the candlelight and the silver dishes, he studied her. She was so beautiful: her hair hung in loose curls around her bare shoulders, above the spaghetti straps of the thin cotton sundress she wore. His pulse raced and pounded.

Abby lifted her chin, pride burning in her eyes. "Clayton, it's too late."

His breathing became shallow as the pressure in his chest increased. Abby wouldn't care what he said—she was leaving. "It's a long overdue apology," he admitted. "I should have…"

Her face paled, all color draining from it. "Colleen told you."

"*You* should have told me."

Abby shook her head. "It was her secret to tell."

"A secret there was no need for."

"Yeah, right," she scoffed. "You wouldn't have screamed and yelled at her…"

"The way I screamed and yelled at you?" Regret and shame weighed heavily on him. He was used to bearing burdens, but his guilt over this particular issue was extremely hard to bear.

"I know you were under a lot of pressure, Clayton. Your dad was dying, and I didn't want to add to that turmoil."

"So you took the blame for something you didn't do." How had he never realized what a wonderful friend, what a wonderful person, she was? Of course, he'd been a little distracted by his sisters' tattoos, which he'd been convinced had been her idea.

"That time, that one thing I didn't do, but I've done plenty of other things I regretted." Her eyes widened with embarrassment. "Not Lara, though. I never regretted my baby."

He rubbed a hand over his chest, remembering how she'd shoved him the night she thought he'd called Lara a mistake. "I know."

"Do you, Clayton? Do you understand what my daughter means to me?"

His heart fell. He didn't want any more responsibility. He didn't want to raise another man's child. But Lara's face, glowing with affection for him, flashed through his mind. "I know."

"She wants to stay in Cloverville."

"So stay."

"Despite keeping Colleen's secret, I'm a selfish person, Clayton." She blew out a breath, causing the curls around her face to dance. "I know what's here for my daughter. But I also want to know what's here for *me*."

As he stepped closer to her, her eyes widened. Instead of reaching for her, he pulled back one of the chairs and held it out for her. "Sit down."

"You think a candlelit dinner will change my mind?" She shook her head. "I'm not a hopeless romantic, Clayton. I'm a practical woman."

"I know. That's why the first course is this." Leaning over her, so close his lips nearly brushed her shoulder, he lifted the cover from a serving platter. A scroll of paper unrolled from the plate.

"What is this?"

"A lease. *I* signed it. It just needs *your* signature." He held out a pen for her.

Her lips curved into a smile. "I don't sign anything without reading it first."

"Of course." He settled into the chair across from her, fascinated as she studied every sentence of the contract. He reached for his glass of wine, sipping from the rim as he watched her. The chardonnay was a poor substitute for her lips. Nothing else was as sweet as Abby's kisses.

She lifted her gaze to his, two lines creasing her brow just above the ridge of her up-turned nose. "It's an open-ended lease."

When he'd decided to take a risk on Abby, he knew he'd have to accept her terms. "As long as you want it, the space is yours."

"Is that giving *me* an out, or *you?*" she asked, her eyes narrowed with suspicion.

Despite the tension in his shoulders, he managed a shrug. "You. I don't want out." But he wasn't sure he could put himself entirely *in,* either.

The paper crinkled as Abby set it aside with a shaking hand. "What do *you* want, Clayton?"

"For you to accept my apology." He swallowed hard, his mouth dry despite the sip of wine he'd just had. "I'm really sorry for the way I've treated you, Abby."

"Are you sorry for kissing me?"

"Abby…"

"Because if you are, you're not going to like this." She stood, ran around the table and tugged him to his feet. Then she threw her arms around his neck, rose up on her toes and pressed her mouth to his. Her lips, soft and warm, tasted as sweet as the cake he'd brought from Kelly's Bakery for dessert. He'd rather have her.

With a groan Clayton pulled back. "I regret a lot of things," he admitted, "but never kissing you. I would have regretted letting you leave."

"I'm not leaving."

Somehow he didn't think she was talking about only Cloverville. "Abby..."

"Shh, Clayton," she said, pressing her fingers against his lips. "Don't say anything that's going to ruin this."

He touched her bare shoulder, fiddling with the thin strap of her shimmery blue dress. "I certainly don't want to ruin this." But he couldn't promise that he wouldn't; he'd never gone this far before with his emotions. He'd never gotten so close to falling in love.

"Then shut up and kiss me!"

His chest shaking with amusement, he pulled her close. In the eight years she'd been gone, Clayton hadn't laughed all that much. And then she'd returned.

Abby stared into Clayton's face. His square jaw relaxed into a wide grin and his eyes shone with a happiness she had never seen before. She couldn't leave Cloverville.

She couldn't leave Clayton.

He held her tight, resting his forehead against

hers. "I don't know why I thought you'd ever be anything but the boss, Abby Hamilton."

"Better the boss than the instigator."

"Troublemaker," he corrected her, as his fingers stroked her shoulders.

She didn't feel like the boss now—she felt totally, happily helpless, as his lips brushed her forehead and then her cheek, before following the angle of her jaw to the sensitive spot below her earlobe. She shivered. "Clayton..."

He was the troublemaker, wreaking havoc with her senses as her pulse raced and her heart beat heavy against her ribs.

"Shh," he murmured. "Shut up and let me kiss you."

His mouth covered hers. Teasing her, he stroked the seam of her lips with his tongue.

Abby moaned, inviting him inside her mouth. And her heart. "Clayton..."

He pulled back and his hands cupped her face, holding her gently, as if she were something delicate and very valuable. "We haven't touched our dinner."

"Forget about food."

"But I'm hungry," he argued, lowering his head. His hair brushed her shoulder as he nipped her earlobe. "I'm hungry for you, Abby.

I haven't slept a night since you set foot back in Cloverville."

"Clayton…"

His lips moved down her throat, and she tipped her head back. Her pulse leapt as his tongue lapped at the pulse point on her neck. He nibbled the ridge of her collarbone while his large, masculine hands carefully slipped the thin straps of her dress down her arms. The cotton skimmed her body and slid off to pool at her feet.

He expelled a ragged breath, then groaned. "You're so damn beautiful."

Self-consciousness tempted her to raise her arms, to cover the curves of her breasts spilling over her strapless demi-bra. But instead she reached for him, untucking his shirt, and then pulling it over his head. She gave in to temptation and ran her hand over the wide expanse of his chest. Muscles rippled beneath her touch.

The clasp of her bra popped, undone by his clever hands, and then the wisp of lingerie dropped to the floor beside her dress. She gasped, her nipples hardening from the intensity of his hot gaze. Then he touched her, using his hands to lift and cup her breasts. He dipped his head to kiss each peak.

When he tugged at a nipple, Abby's knees

weakened and threatened to collapse. She lifted her leg and wrapped it around his hip. His erection, a hard ridge beneath his fly, rubbed against her heat. She moaned as pleasure streaked through her. "Clayton..."

She wanted, she *needed* him to touch her as he had in the hall; to bring her the sweet release she hadn't felt in so long. "Please..."

She wasn't too proud to beg for more, knowing instinctively that he could give her limitless pleasure. He was so used to taking care of others, after all.

And he took care of her. His hands moved down her hips, slipping off her lace panties. Then he settled her onto the cool wooden chair.

"Clayton..." Before she could protest, he dropped to his knees before her. He kissed her first, a deep, penetrating kiss, his tongue slowly and thoroughly stroking hers.

Then he moved his hands along her face, her neck, her shoulders and over her breasts to skim down her sides to her hips and thighs. He lifted her legs over his shoulders, then made love to her with his mouth.

Abby leaned against the hard back of the chair, her body turning to liquid, as with his hands and mouth he brought her a pleasure she'd never reached before. She laced her fingers through his thick hair and moaned his name on her shattering release.

His control snapped as she overwhelmed him. His hands shaking, he shed his pants and boxers. He had to have her. Now. Consumed with desperate need for her, he nearly forgot the condom.

Her eyes wide, she watched him sheathe himself. Then he sat down, lifted her off her chair and settled her onto his lap.

"Clayton, I don't know if we fit."

She was so tight, so hot. He pushed inside her heat.

She bit her lip, her face flushed.

"Am I hurting you?" he asked with concern, stifling a groan as he forced himself to be still.

She shook her head. "Oh, no…" Pleasure poured over him as she came.

"We fit." He'd never expected to say those words about Abby Hamilton. But she fit him. Perfectly. *She* was perfect. He moved, raising his hips as she wriggled on his lap. Her breasts pressed against his chest as she wrapped her arms around his neck.

She lifted her mouth to his, kissing him deeply. Her tongue played with his, tangling.

Clayton moved his hands between them, cupping a breast and flicking his thumb over her nipple as he moved his other hand lower.

She threw her head back and shuddered. This time he came along with her, his fulfillment spilling from his body as he shouted her name. She collapsed against his chest, her head on his shoulder, her silky hair brushing his cheek. He'd never felt so…connected to another person. So complete. "Abby…"

She stiffened, then scrambled off his lap. "Oh, my God," she gasped as she grabbed her dress from the floor. "It's so late!"

"It's not even dark yet," Clayton pointed out, marveling at the way the sun, shining through the high windows of the office, painted her skin—all her bare skin—a deep gold. He groaned as she pulled the dress over her head. "You're not leaving."

"Clayton, I have to go. I have responsibilities."

Yes, he knew about those. He had too many, and now he had two more. Abby and Lara. Not because she'd asked him to assume any responsibility for them, but because Clayton automatically assumed responsibility for the people he loved. Panic pressed against his heart at the realization, paralyzing him so that he couldn't move. He could only watch her walk away.

He loved her.

Chapter Twelve

"You called my mother?" Clayton asked as she walked back into the office, sliding her cell phone into her purse. "What did you tell her?"

He thought she'd left, until he'd come out of his private bathroom and overheard her using the phone in the reception area. Talking to his mom. He could only imagine his matchmaking mother's reaction to Abby's call. She was probably planning his wedding now. Panic pressed on his chest, stealing away his breath like one of Abby's smiles.

She smiled that sassy smile that had always infuriated him, and her blue eyes sparkled mischievously. "I told her the same thing I used to make Colleen and Molly tell her when we were goofing around all night—that I was sleeping over at Brenna's."

Goofing around again. Was that all she thought they were doing? How he wished it were. He didn't want to love *her*. He didn't want to love *anyone*. It wasn't in his plan.

"But you're not sleeping over at Brenna's?" he asked.

"No."

"Then, if you're not going back to my mother's house and you're not going to Brenna's, where are you sleeping, Abby?"

She reached out, linking their fingers together. "Your bed."

She fought to keep the playful grin plastered on her face, not wanting to spook him as she'd spooked herself. When he'd held her in his arms, bringing her pleasure she'd never known until now, she hadn't just lost control of her desire. She'd lost control of her heart, as well.

She'd fallen in love with Clayton McClintock. The realization had scared her so badly she'd felt as if she had to run. But she hadn't gotten far. The foyer. Then, berating herself for being a coward, she'd stopped herself and turned around.

Although his fingers were entwined with hers, he didn't say a word. Maybe he didn't want her. But she wanted him. He stood beside her, so close that she could lean over and kiss his bare chest.

He wore only his pants, low on his lean hips. Her blood rushed through her veins, humming in her ears as desire for his kiss, his touch, consumed her.

Biting her bottom lip to control the urge to tremble, she tipped back her head and stared up into Clayton's face. His eyes serious and dark, he studied her in return.

If he sent her away…

If he told her what they'd just done was all he wanted from her, he would shatter her—she, who'd been so strong for so long, had never been so weak and vulnerable. "Clayton?"

Their hands clasped, his fingers tightened around hers as if he intended to never let her go. "Abby, I…"

She didn't expect a declaration of love. She doubted Clayton could feel about her the way she felt about him. And Clayton, being Clayton, to whom honesty and responsibility meant everything, undoubtedly wanted to make his intentions clear. For example, that he had no intentions other than to lease her his empty office space.

Heat rushed to her face. She'd made a mistake, such a foolish, humiliating mistake. She pulled her hand free of his. "Oh, now I'm the one who made assumptions I shouldn't have. I shouldn't have invited myself…"

"Into my bed?" he teased, his eyes gleaming with mischief.

She smiled, happy he had some mischief in him. "Too presumptuous of me?"

"Abby Hamilton," he murmured, as he toyed with a curl at the curve of her cheek. "You were always in such a hurry."

"I told you I stopped speeding…"

"Maybe in cars, but you're still rushing through life."

Was that his way of telling her that she was pushing too hard? That she wanted more from him than he could give?

He brushed a kiss, whisper-soft, across her lips. "We have all night." He led her back to the table, holding out her chair as if they were dining in an elegant restaurant instead of an empty office.

She struggled to control her emotions,

then settled onto the chair. "Yes, we have all night," she agreed. Probably just tonight. "And your mother would have a fit if she knew we'd let this food go to waste."

Salad with bits of fruit and grilled chicken filled a large bowl on the table, while rolls sat on small plates, butter melted into the flaky layers.

He reached for the wine bottle. "Let me pour you a glass."

"I don't drink."

He shifted the bottle from the rim of her glass and looked at her thoughtfully. The color that had flushed her face earlier drained away. "You've been gone a long time, Abby. There's a lot I don't know about you."

And if he didn't know her, *really* know her, he couldn't love her. He'd only imagined the emotion filling his heart.

"I never drank," she said. "You know *why.*"

Sympathy had him reaching for her hand and squeezing it. She was afraid of being like her mother. "I know what people used to say about your driving…"

Her chin lifted. "They thought I was a drunk, too, and since I came back with Lara, I can guess what else they think about me."

He couldn't begin to imagine how hard it

had been for her to come back to Cloverville. No wonder she'd waited eight long years. "You're nothing like your mother, Abby. The town knows that. And I know that."

She shuddered. "I certainly hope I'm not. I wish I were like your mother."

"A meddling matchmaker?" he teased.

"No."

"You're saying she isn't?"

"Oh, I know she is," she admitted with a laugh. "But she's also a wonderful, loving mother."

"You are, too," he insisted. "Lara is so sweet, so smart. That's because of you."

Abby shook her head, unwilling to accept his compliment. Would she accept his love if he found the strength to offer her his heart? Could he take that big a risk? Could he change his entire plan and make room for a wife, for a child?

Moisture glistened in her eyes, but she blinked away the hint of tears. "She deserves more."

A father? Despite what she'd told him that day outside the hardware store, was Abby looking for a daddy for her daughter?

"She deserves a home and more people than just me to love her."

She did want a father for Lara, which wasn't in Clayton's plan. He'd wanted to put aside the emotional ties and concentrate solely on business. There he could succeed without the risk of pain.

"You're awake."

Abby blinked her eyes open, then squinted against the early-morning light streaming through the blinds on Clayton's bedroom window. This room was as stark as the bedroom of his youth: the outside wall redbrick, the three others white and bare. A mission-style four-poster dominated the room, as Clayton had dominated her mind since she'd found him waiting for her at the airport. "Only just."

Lips slid over her shoulder, raising goose bumps on her skin. "You're cold," a deep voice murmured.

"No…" As the blanket slipped down her body, she grabbed at it, knotting her fingers in the soft wool. But Clayton was stronger. He pulled the coverings free of her body, leaving her lying naked in the middle of his bed. "Clayton…"

Muscles that Abby hadn't known she had ached. She'd never been made love to so thoroughly before. She'd never been made love to; her few experiences had been only about sex.

His lips and hands skimmed over her body, heating her skin. A gasp of pleasure slipped from between her lips as he caressed her. Because he was a generous man, she'd known he'd be a generous lover. But she'd had no idea how much he could give her.

Now she wanted him to take. She pushed him onto his back, then swung her leg across his hips so that she straddled him. Her breath caught, desire flooding her as his erection nudged her backside. But this time wasn't about her, unlike all the other times they'd made love last night. This time was for him. Her lips clung to his before sliding over the hard, stubbled line of his square jaw. Then she nibbled the straining cords of his neck.

He groaned. Until the nip of her teeth against his skin, he'd thought he'd been dreaming. Awakening with Abby, naked in his rumpled sheets, felt like a dream. One he'd had so long he'd been convinced it would always go unfulfilled.

Like the dream, the plan, he had had since he was a little boy visiting his father's office, of one day running the insurance agency with his dad. Instead, he'd had to manage alone.

He'd thought he'd live his personal life the same way he had his professional one. Alone. Until now. Until Abby Hamilton made love to him.

Her hands and mouth moved over him, bringing him a pleasure he'd never dreamed existed, giving him more than he'd ever received. He tried to topple her off, to take back control. But Abby drove him out of his mind, her lips sliding over every inch of him. He fisted his hand in her tangled curls, pulling her up before he completely unraveled.

Then he lifted her, plunging into her wet heat. "Abby!"

She moved her hips and arched her back, taking him deeper. His hands skimmed up her body, cupping her breasts. His thumbs flicked over her nipples. Then he lifted up to close his lips over one of the hard points, tugging with his mouth and nipping with his teeth.

"Clayton!" she screamed as she came apart in his arms.

Her muscles squeezed him, her pleasure flooding him. She shuddered against him, falling to his chest. He clasped her close and rolled with her, still connected. He buried himself in her, deeper and deeper, until his world shattered. "Abby!"

He rolled them again, so that she lay atop, sprawled across him. She buried her head against his shoulder, her breath warm against his neck. "You know what this means, right?"

Panic knotted his stomach. He'd forgotten a condom. For the first time ever, he'd forgotten to use a condom. He, the man who'd been obsessive about taking on *no* more responsibility. What had he done?

"What?" he repeated aloud.

"I need to sneak out of here."

"What?" She hadn't yet realized that he hadn't used a condom. Or maybe she didn't care because, after having Lara, she'd undoubtedly gone on some kind of protection.

He forced himself to relax. For now. But he'd ask her about it later, when he could draw a breath without gasping. God, she was incredible.

"I can't believe I lied to your mother," she murmured against his throat. "She's going to think…"

His gut clenched. She was going to think she'd finally get some grandchildren from him. And she might be right.

"The whole town's going to think…"

"You want to go out the window?" he teased, oddly touched by her embarrassment. He wouldn't have figured Abby Hamilton cared anymore what the town thought of her. "I can tie some sheets together."

She slapped her palm against his shoulder. "Come on. You know Cloverville. If I walk out of this building at the crack of dawn, someone's going to see me."

He nodded. "Most likely Mrs. Hild." He glanced at his watch. "She's usually working in her front garden about now. Or Mr. Carpenter. He's probably redoing those windows. You left all kinds of soap streaks on them."

"I was distracted."

"Yeah, I understand that," he said as his gaze slid over her naked skin like a caress.

"Hey, we just…"

The theme from *Charlie's Angels* pealed out of the purse that Abby had dropped next to the bed last night. She pulled away from Clayton, her breasts skimming his chest as she rolled onto the other side of the mattress. Then she leaned over to fumble inside her bag. Warm lips slid over her back, trailing kisses down her spine. Goose bumps rose along her skin and she squirmed on the sheets. Her hand trembled, nearly dropping the phone she pulled from her purse. "Clayton…"

"Let it go to voice mail," he murmured between kisses on the small of her back, the curve of her hip.

How could he want her again? So soon? The man was insatiable.

"I…" She glimpsed the number on the caller ID. "I have to take this."

She flipped on her cell. "Hello?"

"Abby? Where are you?"

"Where are you is the question everyone's been asking," she teased the runaway bride.

"I'm…"

"I know."

"You know where I've been?"

"The minute you went out the window we all had a pretty good idea where you'd taken off to," she admitted. "But you wanted time alone to figure out what you want. Did you figure it out?"

"Yes," Molly admitted.

A sigh drew Abby's attention to where Clayton stood beside the bed, clad only in a pair of black boxers. She thought he'd gone into the bathroom. But, then, he hadn't had a condom to dispose of. Clayton, who wanted no more responsibility in his life, had failed to act responsibly?

Not that condoms were foolproof. Lara was proof that they weren't, so Abby had gone on the Pill, even though she hadn't needed birth control since Lara's birth. She'd been so careful, so unwilling to trust anyone with her heart. Until now.

"Abby?" Molly called out, her voice screeching in the phone. "Are you there?"

"Yes." Naked and vulnerable in Clayton's bed, desperate for any indication that he might love her. "Are *you* all right?" She already knew she, herself, wasn't.

"I'm fine." Molly's sigh rattled the phone. "Just embarrassed and sorry."

"It's okay. You did what you had to do." And so would Abby. "Everyone will understand."

Molly's voice softened to a whisper. "I'm not so sure about that."

"If you're worried about Clayton…"

"I'm not worried about Clayton. He thrives on damage control," she said, dismissing her brother's feelings.

Abby had called Rory on his disregard for Clayton. She would call Molly on it, too—when Clayton wasn't listening.

"I'm worried about you," Molly continued.

"Me?"

Did she know what Abby had gone and done? Cloverville was a small town, and since Molly hadn't left it, she might know how much time Abby had spent with her big brother. She might even know about last night.

"I know how much you hated coming back," Molly said. "I'm sorry I asked you to stay. That was so selfish of me."

"I wasn't staying just because you asked me to," she admitted. She hadn't been staying to launch a business or to make her daughter happy, either. She'd been staying to see if Clayton could love her. Had she wasted her time?

"Good, because I don't want you to stay, if there's someplace you'd rather be."

"No." There was no place she'd rather be than in Clayton's bed, in Clayton's arms. But did he want her there? For keeps?

"I'm fine," Molly insisted, a little too adamantly.

She wasn't fine. But neither was Abby. Her heart beat heavy with dread as Clayton held out his hand for the phone. "Let me talk to my sister," he insisted.

Abby passed over her cell. As their fingers brushed, she shivered. Instead of the usual heat, his touch left her cold this time, like the disillusioned look in his eyes as he met her gaze before turning away. Clasping the sheet to her breasts with one hand, she pulled her rumpled sundress over her head with the other. But she needn't have worried about modesty. Clayton had his back to her as he spoke to his sister in the low, soft tone that he would use with a frightened child; that he'd used with Lara, charming his way into her daughter's heart as he had Abby's. Or had he always been there?

"It's okay," he assured Molly. "Mom turned the reception into a welcome-home party for Abby and Lara."

Molly's laugh filled his ear. "Home? Abby will never consider Cloverville home. She hated living here. I was wrong to ask her to stay until I sorted my head out."

"Did you?" he asked.

"Yeah, in the note I left her."

So once again Abby had acted out of her loyalty to her friend, not her interest in *him*. "No, did you sort your head out?"

"Yes."

"Then you did the right thing, taking time to figure things out." He needed time, too, but he hadn't had any to himself in the past eight years. "So are you coming home?"

"Yes, I'll explain everything then." Molly's breath caught as she said, "I'm sorry."

"Don't worry," he said. Then he lied to her. "Everything's fine."

After saying goodbye to his sister, he handed the cell back to Abby, who'd pulled on her sundress. She stood before him, her face bare of makeup, her hair tangled around her shoulders, and she'd never been more beautiful to him. And he'd never felt so weak and helpless.

To protect himself, he had to lash out. "You knew where she was all along! You knew I was worried about her, but you didn't tell me!"

"She wanted to be alone to think. She couldn't do that with you around, pressuring her."

Sure, he understood pressure; it pushed down on his chest, stealing his breath. "You should have told me."

"I couldn't betray my friendship with Molly."

"Like you couldn't betray Colleen and tell me the truth eight years ago when I was blaming you?"

"Isn't that what you're doing now?" she asked, her voice so quiet it stopped his rant more effectively than a shout. "Don't you want to blame *me* for your pulling away?"

She'd been gone eight years. How did she

know him so well? Her intuitiveness increased his fear about falling for her. He wouldn't be able to keep anything from her; he had no protection from her. But his pride. "I blame myself."

She lifted her chin—pride was one of the things they had in common. Skepticism narrowing her eyes, she asked, "You blame yourself?"

"For trusting you. I should have known better." He struggled to control his voice and his emotions, saying, "You were only sticking around for Molly. Because she asked you to stay."

She shook her head. "That wasn't the only reason."

"For the business?"

She shook her head again, then drew in a loud, deep breath and said, "For you. I love you, Clayton."

Stunned, Clayton rubbed a hand over his unshaven jaw, holding it as if she'd punched him. And maybe she had. He certainly deserved it.

Tears burned Abby's eyes, but she blinked them away, refusing to cry over him. She grabbed her purse from the floor and stepped into her shoes, ready to run. "Don't worry about…"

But he caught her and held her tight, his hands warm against her skin. "I care about you, Abby. About you and Lara."

Care. Bitterness and regret rose in her throat, choking her. She'd really thought he'd be different. "Thanks…"

"That's why I think you and your daughter deserve more, Abby. I don't have enough to offer anyone. I'm so busy."

"So busy or so scared?" she challenged him.

"Abby, you don't understand."

"Then explain it to me."

"I have this plan."

He'd always had a plan. She remembered the lists she used to find when she'd snooped in his bedroom. "I know, you said there's no room in your plan for a wife or kids."

But she'd hoped he would change the plan. For her. Was that what she wanted? Someone else to resent her intrusion in his life? She shook her head. "No, you're right. I don't want to mess up your plans. I know from experience that you'd only come to hate me…"

He hugged her. "I could never hate you, Abby."

She pulled herself clear of his arms. "Really? I think I could hate you, if I hung around here, if I kept hoping for more. That's why I'm leaving. Today."

"What about…" The color drained from his face. "Is it possible… You and I didn't use anything this last time. Can you be…?"

She laughed, despite the pain closing in on her heart. He wanted no connection to her. Just as she had been wrong about Lara's father, she'd been wrong about Clayton, too; believing him to be the *one* man who wouldn't want to simply use her and toss her aside.

"Don't worry about having another responsibility, Clayton," she said, her lips twisting in a bitter smile. "I take care of myself. I always have."

"Abby…"

"And don't worry about the lease," she said as she headed toward the door, her legs shaking. "I never signed it."

How was she ever going to make it out of the room and down the stairs? How was she ever going to walk away from him?

She'd thought her heart broke years ago, when Mr. McClintock died and she'd had to keave all her friends behind in Cloverville.

But she'd had no idea then how much pain she could feel, as she finally accepted the truth.

Clayton would never be able to love her in the way that she loved him. And she deserved more.

She deserved *love*.

Chapter Thirteen

"No!" Lara shouted in protest. "I'm not leaving. You can't make me leave!" Then she hurled her favorite stuffed animal, a fuzzy black teddy bear, at her mother, and ran from the guest room.

Her hands trembling, Abby leaned over and picked up the bear. Her sweet child, who had never—in almost five years—thrown a tantrum, had chosen today of all days to act out? Abby sunk onto the mattress next to her empty suitcase, which shifted and dug into her hip. Really, Mrs. Mick had to stop unpacking her suitcase.

She had changed out of her rumpled sundress, unable to bear the scent of Clayton that clung to it, that clung to her skin despite her shower. She breathed deep, inhaling his particular mix of citrus and musk, a scent that was his alone.

"Are you okay?" asked a warm, maternal voice.

Abby turned toward the doorway, blinking back the tears blurring her eyes, so that she could face Mrs. Mick. "I'm sorry," she murmured.

"For what, honey?"

She pressed the heels of her hands over her eyes, trying to push back the tears. She couldn't keep crying. She hated crying—even Mrs. Mick's so-called *good* cries. "I lied to you." Her breath hitched. "I didn't stay at Brenna's."

The mattress lifted. The suitcase dropped to the floor with a thud, and then the mattress shifted again as Mrs. Mick settled next to Abby, her arm wrapped supportively around her shoulders. "I know."

She kept her face buried in her hands. "You knew where I was?"

"With Clayton," Mrs. McClintock confirmed, then chuckled. "I'm a mother, honey. Mothers know everything."

Only real mothers like Mary McClintock.

"I didn't know how crushed Lara would be that we have to leave," she admitted. "I knew she was getting attached…"

She waited for motherly advice. For Mrs. Mick to assure her that she just had to give the little girl time. That was why she'd let her run off without chasing her. Lara needed some distance. And so did Abby, from Clayton.

But Mrs. McClintock withdrew her arm and her support. "You don't have to leave."

Abby nodded. "I do," she insisted. "I do." Before she buried her pride and begged Clayton to take her on his terms. But he probably wouldn't have her even then—she wasn't part of his plan. He couldn't make room for her in his life, in his heart. "I need you to drive me to the airport."

"No."

"But I don't have a car." She was so desperate to leave Cloverville that she'd ask Rory to drive her, but he didn't even have a permit yet. "And I need to get out of here."

"No," Mrs. McClintock said again, just that one word, her voice more stern than Abby had ever heard her. She shook her head, her brown eyes, usually so warm, darkened with disappointment.

"I don't know what you thought. That Clayton and I…" She swallowed the threat of a sob. "That we… We can't get along. Even before his dad died, he was overbearing. He's used to bossing everyone around."

His mother didn't defend him. She didn't say anything. She just let Abby rant.

"I've been on my own too long. I take care of myself. Clayton has to take care of everyone around him. He says he doesn't want to…" She slapped a hand over her mouth, horrified about what she'd revealed. "I shouldn't have said that. I…"

"I know my son," Mrs. McClintock reminded Abby. "I know what he did when his father was dying. How he threw himself into his schoolwork, so he could graduate early. Then he threw himself into the business and into his family's lives. Do you know why he did that?"

Abby shrugged but actually she knew. She understood Clayton, too. That was why she loved him. "He thought that he was honoring his father by taking care of everyone the way his dad had."

A tear streaked down the older woman's cheek. "Partly. He loved his father very much."

Abby nodded. "I know."

"Do you know he never cried? Not once did he cry when his father was sick, not even when he died." Mary McClintock's breath was ragged. "I think all I did was cry then."

"He was being strong," Abby said, defending the man she loved. "He was supporting all of you."

"He was scared," Mrs. McClintock said. "He was scared to let himself feel, scared of the pain. That's why he did whatever he did this morning to push you away. He's scared to feel the love that I *know* he has for you."

Panic pressed against Abby's chest. She couldn't believe the older woman, she couldn't hope for something she'd already accepted that there would never be. "I love you, Mrs. Mick, but you're wrong."

"Abby Hamilton…"

"No," she said, using the sharp tone she used only when reprimanding lazy workers or admonishing demanding clients. "I can't." She scrambled off the bed to pick up her suitcase. "I need a ride to the airport. If you won't drive me, I'll call a cab."

"You need to stop running, Abby Hamilton," Mrs. McClintock said, shaking her head as her eyes filled with tears of disappointment. "You've been running eight years, but you can't leave Cloverville. It's in your heart, just like Clayton is."

"I don't… I can't."

"I didn't think I could, either," Clayton's mother admitted. "That I could love another man."

Abby had only loved one man—a man who couldn't love her back because he was scared to feel. "You're seeing someone?"

As the older woman smiled, her eyes brightened with a warmth that emanated from her heart. "Martin Schipper."

"Mr. Schipper." He'd failed Abby two years in a row. Of course, back in school, she'd never been able to concentrate long enough to finish reading a book and turn in the required reports.

"He's a good man, and I almost let him get away." She sighed. "Because I was scared."

Mrs. Mick had always seemed so strong, even when her beloved husband had been sick. Or maybe most especially then.

"I was scared of the pain that I might feel if I cared about someone and lost him again." She shook her head, as if disappointed in herself. "Then I realized that it was better to feel pain than nothing at all. Stop running, Abby.

Everything you want is right here. Be strong enough to fight for it."

"I don't want to fight Clayton," she said, smiling despite her pain. For so many years that was all they'd done.

"You two need each other. I thought that was true eight years ago. I know it for a fact now. You balance each other."

Abby bit her lip and shook her head.

"You have a lot to think about. I'm going to take Lara to the park for a little while."

"I'm leaving," she interrupted, desperation clawing at her throat, choking her with emotion.

"If you still want to leave when Lara and I get back, I'll drive you," Mrs. McClintock offered before turning away and leaving Abby alone to think.

Abby's head and heart hurt too much for thinking. She could only react. She pulled out the drawer of the bedside table, finding Mrs. Mick actually had stocked it like a hotel room, with a Bible and a phone book. With trembling fingers, she leafed through the yellow pages for cab companies.

Clayton's gut tightened so much that he nearly doubled over in pain as he stood on the sidewalk and watched the cab pull away from his family house. Taking Abby and Lara to the airport, away from him.

He'd been such a fool. But he'd already driven her away, or she wouldn't have called that cab. He should be relieved. He didn't need any more stress in his life, anyone else to worry about. He already had more than he could handle, and even if he didn't he would never be able to handle Abby Hamilton.

But yet he'd run all the way from town. Not to stop her from leaving. He knew he had nothing to offer her to make her stay, just the lease she hadn't signed. He owed her an apology though. She hadn't betrayed him by not revealing Molly's whereabouts. She'd been loyal, just as she'd always been, to her friends, the people who'd earned her loyalty.

Clayton, having always been unfair to her, had done nothing to deserve her loyalty. Or her love. He couldn't expect her to stay in Cloverville where, as she'd feared, there was nothing for her.

Still he owed her that apology. His legs leaden, not from his run but with dread, he walked up the drive to his house and pulled open the screen door of the kitchen. His mother would have Abby's cell number. All these years they'd kept in close contact. He could only imagine how disappointed she'd be that he'd hurt Abby. Again.

"Ouch," yelped a feminine voice as a head cracked against his chin in the kitchen doorway.

Strong hands closed around Abby's upper arms, holding her steady as stars danced before her eyes. Then the stars flickered out and disappeared, leaving only Clayton's face, his eyes shining brighter than any of them. She'd been about to head for town, to confront him, after sending away the cab and calling Mrs. Mick to keep Lara occupied a while longer.

"I'm not leaving," she blurted out.

"But I saw the cab…"

"I'm not leaving," she repeated, and as she said it, she accepted that she'd come *home,* to stay. No matter what happened with Clayton. But she'd wear him down—if not today, eventually.

"I'm sorry," he said.

The apology struck her like a slap, and she drew in a quick breath.

"Not that you're staying," he said, his words rushing together. "I'm sorry for how I treated you."

With more tenderness and generosity than

she'd ever known? Mrs. Mick was right. Clayton loved her. While he hadn't admitted it in words, he'd betrayed himself with his actions. *He loved her.*

He cupped her face in his hands, brushing away the tears that streamed from her eyes. His voice thick with misery, he said again, "I'm so sorry. I never meant to hurt you."

"I know," she said. "You love me."

His hands dropped from her face and he stepped back, banging into the screen door that had closed behind him, trapping him in the kitchen with her.

Abby's smile grew. Who was running now? "*You* love *me*," she repeated.

He shook his head. "I was honest with you. I have so much… I can't…"

"Take on any more responsibility?" she finished for him, her confidence growing. "I know. You were honest with me. It's yourself you're lying to, Clayton McClintock."

"Abby."

"I've been taking care of myself for eight years and Lara for the last four." Only today had she failed her child, hurting her needlessly. But Lara was a sweetheart, and she would forgive her mother. Clayton needed to forgive himself. "I worked my way through school, and started my own successful business. I don't need anyone to take care of me."

She was right, of course. She didn't need him. While the thought should have filled him with relief, his heart clenched with regret instead.

"*I* can take care of *you*." Despite her words, she didn't wear her sassy smile. Her eyes didn't twinkle with that mischievous glint. She was serious.

Clayton swallowed hard, choking on emotion, but he couldn't accept Abby's words. She grabbed his hand, her fingers twining with his, and she tugged him down the hall.

They must be alone in the house if she was leading him toward the stairs. To her bed? His body tensed, hardening with need for her. Even after all the times they'd made love this morning and the night before, he wanted her again. Still. Always.

But she stopped at the doorway to his father's den. "If you ever want to move on, Clayton, you have to go back." She blew out an unsteady breath. "I realize that now that I'm back home. I was running. From the past… and the future. I could never fall in love because my heart was always here. With you."

"But I was never nice to you," he reminded

her, concerned that she'd painted him in some romantic light when he really belonged in the dark.

"You weren't much older than me, but you were so *responsible*." She said the last word wistfully, as if it were something special, as if *he* were something special. "You know how I grew up, with parents who were everything but responsible. They didn't care about me, and I was their only child."

Fortunately they hadn't had any more. Some people couldn't handle responsibility. Most of the time Clayton suspected he was one of those people. He'd managed the business. But Rory and Molly and Colleen...

"But you," she continued, "you cared about everyone. You took care of everyone."

"But you," he reminded her.

"You tried. You stopped me from getting that tattoo."

Which he'd occasionally regretted.

"I didn't like you then," she admitted. "But I think I must have already begun to fall in love with you. That's why I took a chance on Lara's dad. He reminded me of you. But he wasn't."

Because he'd hurt her. He'd let her down. Clayton's gut twisted into knots as he worried that he would, too. "I'm sorry," he said. She deserved happiness, real happiness.

And so did he.

He passed her in the doorway, stepping into his father's den for the first time in eight years. Abby squeezed his hand. He hadn't even realized their fingers were still interlaced. She was like that, already wrapped around his heart. He couldn't let her go.

But she was right. He had to face the past in order to have a future.

Don't be so hard on that poor girl, his father's voice, weak from fighting cancer but strong with conviction, echoed in the room. He'd known Abby wasn't responsible for the accident. He must have known she'd been covering for Colleen. He hadn't left this room, his bed, in so long, but still he'd seemed to know everything that had gone on in his family's lives and hearts. *You'll regret it, if you drive her away.*

Tears stung eyes that had remained dry all through his father's final battle. Even after his father had lost, Clayton hadn't cried. He'd held his sisters and his mom when they'd wept. But he'd never shed a tear over his father's passing.

"Why do you want *me,* Abby?" he asked. "I'm a cold, unfeeling…"

She pressed her fingers against his lips. "Shut up," she said, tears streaking down her face. "Don't talk that way about the man I love."

"Abby, I don't deserve you."

"No, you don't," she agreed with him. Finally.

"But I'm not letting you go," he said. He pulled her into his arms, holding her tight against his heart. He was a man, despite the damage her knee had almost done to him in the alley a few days earlier, and so he fought the tears. But they fell, slipping silently down his face as he finally let go of his grief. Instead of feeling the pain he'd feared, his heart lifted, filled with joy, with love.

"It's a good cry," Abby murmured as she dried his face with her hands and her lips. "It's a good cry."

Clayton pulled away from her, and Abby feared she'd pushed him too far, too hard. He couldn't deal with everything she'd thrown at him. Reeling from his past, he couldn't contemplate a future.

She sucked in a shaky breath, bracing herself to offer him time. She wasn't leaving. She could wait.

But wood creaked beneath his feet as he

walked across the floor, then at the desk as he pulled open a drawer. "You made yourself at home, huh?" he murmured, gesturing toward her in/out box and the shelves she'd put up behind the desk.

She nodded, regretting how she'd intruded on what, to Clayton, must have felt like a sacred place. "I'm sorry."

"Don't be. Don't ever be sorry," he said as he pulled something from the drawer. His big hand swallowed the little box, hiding it from her view until he walked back to her and dropped to one knee. Then he showed the velvet case to her, opened to reveal the contents—a gold ring with a single oval diamond winking up at her.

"My father left me this," he said. "I think he hoped that someday I'd give it to you."

"Clayton…" Emotion overwhelmed her, and more tears poured from her eyes.

Was he proposing?

"It's old and the diamond was all he could afford at the time, when he was just starting up the business. So he replaced it years later, on their twenty-fifth wedding anniversary, with a bigger stone. I could get you another one if you'd prefer."

Abby shook her head. She knew exactly what

that ring symbolized—the all-encompassing love his parents had felt for each other. The love she felt for Clayton.

"No, you don't want another, or no, you don't want this ring, either?"

She blinked to clear her eyes, and then she rested her hands on his shoulders, squeezing in frustration. "What the hell are you asking me?"

He laughed. "I'm asking you to marry me."

"Why?" For so long she'd made a policy of asking no one for anything. Maybe that was why she was greedy now. She wanted it all.

"Because I love you," he said. "And I love Lara." He sighed, as if his heart had swelled so much that he couldn't contain the emotion. "I didn't want to, but she's so damn adorable. So special. I won't let you or her down, Abby. I'll be a good father to her. A good husband to you. I promise."

"Oh, Clayton, you're better than good," she assured him, wrapping her arms tight around his neck. "You're perfect!"

"Is that a yes?" he asked, his voice muffled as his head was buried in her chest.

"Oh, yes."

He rose to his feet then, clasping her to him with one arm while he spun her around. "Yes!" he shouted. "Yes!"

"Spin me!" a soft voice demanded as Lara rushed into the room with them. "Spin me!"

When he set her down, dizziness washed over Abby, lightening her head while her heart filled. Tears streaked her face again as she watched Clayton pick up her daughter and hold her close. Like her mother, Lara's wish had been fulfilled, too. She had her daddy.

"See," Mrs. Mick said, her arm sliding around Abby's shoulders and squeezing. "You all belong together."

Abby nodded in heartfelt agreement. "Yes, we do."

Epilogue

The bridesmaids wore strapless red dresses; the bride wore white, despite having one child already and another on the way, a barely perceptible bump beneath the empire waistline of the lacy dress. *Let 'em talk.* Abby Hamilton was used to the Cloverville busybodies gossiping about her; she wouldn't have it any other way. Better to be known by everyone in town than be invisible, the way she'd been in the big cities where she'd spent the past eight years.

Molly, wearing Abby's old bridesmaid gown, walked over to the window of the dressing room and lifted the sash. "Want to make a break for it?"

The breeze ruffled Abby's veil, brushing the lace against her cheek as she joined her matron of honor at the window. Her hands over Molly's, she closed the sash. "No way."

When she'd come back to Cloverville a few months ago, she hadn't imagined that the wedding she'd returned for would be her own. To Clayton McClintock, of all people.

"Do you have everything?" Brenna, who always mothered everyone, had to ask.

Abby laughed as she patted the soft swell of her belly. Birth control had failed her once more. But she couldn't be happier. She reminded her friend, "I'm not exactly your traditional bride."

But she'd borrowed her wedding dress from Molly. She wore something blue—a garter that she couldn't wait for Clayton to remove. The something old actually had been a gift, another slip of paper but not a lease—it was the deed to the McClintock house. Mrs. Mick, Mom, had given them the house as a wedding present, since she and Rory were moving in with her new husband, Mr. Schipper.

Abby would raise her daughter and the children she and Clayton would have together in the house in which she'd always wished she'd grown up. In which she actually *had* grown up, the day she'd stopped running.

The something new wasn't her love for Clayton, because she suspected she'd already loved him a long time but their commitment to each other was new.

"Mommy! Hurry up," Lara demanded as she stood at the door, clad again in her miniature wedding dress. Such a careful, thoughtful child, there was not one speck of dust or cake on the pristine white dress despite the number of times she'd worn it.

How had Abby produced such an angel? She already had a streak of red lipstick on the bodice of her gown, from when she'd fumbled with her makeup before Colleen had taken over the task of making her beautiful.

She needn't have bothered. As Rory led her down the aisle to her groom, she realized she'd feel beautiful in Clayton's eyes no matter what. He waited for her at the altar, his expression bright with love as he watched her walk toward him.

She slipped her arm free of Rory's, then passed him the bouquet. The teenager fumbled with the white and red flowers. "Abby, what…"

Then she dug her hands into the satin and

lace, gathering up the folds of the long white gown so she wouldn't trip, and ran toward her groom. A murmur rose above the notes of the wedding march Mrs. Hild played. Then laughter swelled above the music.

Lara, standing on the side of the altar next to the bridesmaids, shook her head. "Mama, you're not s'pose to run in church."

Mr. Carpenter, sitting toward the front of the church, had discarded his tool apron for an ill-fitting green suit. Slicked back, his gray hair didn't move when he turned toward his wife and shook his head. "That's Abby Hamilton for you," his big voice boomed, his hearing aid screeching in accompaniment to the piano. "Always in a hurry!"

She was in a hurry—to become Abby *McClintock*. She slipped her hand into Clayton's, who squeezed her fingers. "I love you. I'll love you forever."

"I love you," he said, a smile of pure joy illuminating his handsome face. "I'll love you forever."

While they said the rest, those were the vows that mattered, the vows that would bind them together forever as husband and wife.

* * * * *

HOMETOWN HEARTS ♡

YES! Please send me **The Hometown Hearts Collection** in Larger Print. This collection begins with 3 FREE books and 2 FREE gifts in the first shipment. Along with my 3 free books, I'll also get the next 4 books from the Hometown Hearts Collection, in LARGER PRINT, which I may either return and owe nothing, or keep for the low price of $4.99 U.S./ $5.89 CDN each plus $2.99 for shipping and handling per shipment*. If I decide to continue, about once a month for 8 months I will get 6 or 7 more books, but will only need to pay for 4. That means 2 or 3 books in every shipment will be FREE! If I decide to keep the entire collection, I'll have paid for only 32 books because 19 books are FREE! I understand that accepting the 3 free books and gifts places me under no obligation to buy anything. I can always return a shipment and cancel at any time. My free books and gifts are mine to keep no matter what I decide.

262 HCN 3432 462 HCN 3432

Name	(PLEASE PRINT)	
Address		Apt. #
City	State/Prov.	Zip/Postal Code

Signature (if under 18, a parent or guardian must sign)

Mail to the **Reader Service:**
IN U.S.A.: P.O. Box 1867, Buffalo, NY. 14240-1867
IN CANADA: P.O. Box 609, Fort Erie, Ontario L2A 5X3

HHBPA17

Get 2 Free Books,
Plus 2 Free Gifts—
just for trying the Reader Service!

HRLP17R

Get 2 Free Books,
Plus 2 Free Gifts—
just for trying the Reader Service!

YES! Please send me 2 FREE Harlequin® Special Edition novels and my 2 FREE gifts (gifts are worth about $10 retail). After receiving them, if I don't wish to receive any more books, I can return the shipping statement marked "cancel." If I don't cancel, I will receive 6 brand-new novels every month and be billed just $4.99 per book in the U.S. or $5.74 per book in Canada. That's a savings of at least 12% off the cover price! It's quite a bargain! Shipping and handling is just 50¢ per book in the U.S. and 75¢ per book in Canada.* I understand that accepting the 2 free books and gifts places me under no obligation to buy anything. I can always return a shipment and cancel at any time. Even if I never buy another book, the 2 free books and gifts are mine to keep forever.

235/335 HDN GLP5

Name _____ (PLEASE PRINT)

Address _____ Apt. #

City _____ State/Province _____ Zip/Postal Code

Signature (if under 18, a parent or guardian must sign)

Mail to the **Reader Service:**
IN U.S.A.: P.O. Box 1867, Buffalo, NY 14240-1867
IN CANADA: P.O. Box 611, Fort Erie, Ontario L2A 9Z9

Want to try two free books from another line?
Call 1-800-873-8635 or visit www.ReaderService.com.

Get 2 Free Books,
Plus 2 Free Gifts—
just for trying the
Reader Service!

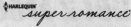

Get 2 Free Books,
Plus 2 Free Gifts—
just for trying the Reader Service!

HARLEQUIN

HEARTWARMING™

HW17

Get 2 Free Books,
<u>Plus</u> 2 Free Gifts -
just for trying the *Reader Service!*

READERSERVICE.COM

Manage your account online!

- Review your order history
- Manage your payments
- Update your address

We've designed the Reader Service website just for you.

Enjoy all the features!

- Discover new series available to you, and read excerpts from any series.
- Respond to mailings and special monthly offers.
- Browse the Bonus Bucks catalog and online-only exculsives.
- Share your feedback.

Visit us at:

ReaderService.com

RS16R